INTRODUCTION

Nothing is ever wasted when it comes to writing; it is merely work in progress.

The first few short stories in this collection evolved from messy attempts at funny blogs and short story competitions, when I had two breakdowns and struggled to stay sane. In fact, I would say that writing was my lifeboat through those choppy seas of rejections and successes and kept me afloat for many years . . .

A Dress for a Queen had so many rewrites I've lost count.

It was one of the first things I ever wrote. I remember writing it and thinking how funny I was and what wonderful sentences I had written.

The plot, however, sucked.

It was longlisted for a prize, which I dined out on for years, spurring me to keep trying. In the end, it took me years of experience to mold this story into something that works.

The Story That Got Away comes from a time years ago when I worked in an office and was bored out of my brain. I spent my spare time (of which there was plenty) working on *Thirty Seconds*, a novel that in the end never saw the light of day, mainly because the plot, yet again, sucked. I had no idea what I was doing, I was obsessed with creating jokes. However, years later, those characters rose to the occasion, some finding their way into my Diva Diaries Novella series and another here in *The Story That Got Away*.

Mavis and Me "Do" Half-Life was my first commission. While working in said office, I had my first breakdown that led to lots of walking in hilly winds. At the time, there were several outdoor art exhibitions created on ancient stone sites in the area and an outdoor play that was so *arty* I had no idea what it was about. The exhibition, "Half Life," ran for a month, and I (being a local writer) was asked to add something to the "Half Life" booklet, which gave me free access to everything, including the drinks *do* afterwards.

Halloween and Christmas Lights was born from the *Nefertiti Has Her Say* blog. This was my first blog, which I would say is pretty rubbish; the plotting is all over the place (some would say nonexistent). However, Nefertiti's voice really developed in those good old blogging days, and despite a second breakdown, that blog led to a second novel, *The Downfall of a Belly Dancer*, along with my short story *Halloween and Christmas Lights*.

Boudicca and Mavis is another born-again story rewritten many times. It comes from a real-life event: me on a papier mâché horse for an autumn festival. So much of that story is true, although I'm not telling which part, except I did have a beard painted on and, thank God, no one recognised me.

The Red Cross Shop and the Codpiece is a wee piece inspired by teaching belly dancing to a local guild group years ago.

The group stopped midway through for coffee and to judge their very own craft table, amongst which were two crochet-covered coat hangers. Those women took more time judging the craft table than learning to shimmy, and I couldn't help thinking there was a story in there somewhere.

Plus, I am a real sucker for second-hand shops.

A DRESS FOR A QUEEN

Every queen has a secret life, even those with a respectable accent.

The Secret Apprentice

Lizzie's favourite pastimes were juggling and acrobatics, which she loved to do while sliding down a banister or swinging from a chandelier. After dinner, before the servants even had a chance to grab a tray let alone clear the debris, Lizzie was on the table spinning plates and tossing cups—oblivious to the flying food.

The rest of the family ducked . . .

"Watch out, lovers," Lizzie would shout in her best Cockney voice before propelling herself onto the nearest light fitting and swinging across the room. The family, grabbing their whisky, would scatter like dogs on a hunt.

She loved to cartwheel, somersault, and juggle, sometimes together. She practiced in the kitchen when the servants had finished, in the garden when the sun was down, and in the reception on the footman's day off, always concluding with a few splits. Lizzie liked to end with panache.

All it took was one vodka, a gin, or a couple of glasses of bubbly and Lizzie, roots forgotten, became the real Lizzie: an adrenaline junkie who loved to shock.

And it was all thanks to Jimmie Black, a distant cousin . . .

Jimmie Black had left the family business after an embarrassing incident with the gamekeeper. He joined a circus, and Lizzie wanted to follow; she was a teenager at the time and thought she knew all there was to know about bunking off.

"I'm sick," she moaned to her nanny and took to her bed.

Later, with the good ol' pillows-in-the-bed trick and a "Lizzie is at death's door" note on her bedroom door, Lizzie escaped. She slid on her red *Annie* wig, pulled on an off-the-peg dress from the Lost Properties Department at the palace, and slid into the night.

That night, as she watched the jugglers and the trapeze artists, Lizzie fell in love. She too wanted to balance on the back of a white stallion in a frilly skirt, swing from the tent tops, and feel the heat of a fire stick as she twirled it about her plump body. She discovered a passion for performing deeper than any feelings for her family—or "the Firm," as some called them—until her nanny found her.

Lizzie, posed at the front row clutching a bag of leotards, didn't see her coming. She didn't recognise the plump woman in a grey tracksuit, the smell of mothballs, or the face beneath the knitted hat. *Nanny also knew about the Lost Properties Department.*

"Leotards are not for the likes of you," the nanny finally whispered, and the incident was never spoken of again.

The Honeymoon and Beyond

After her marriage to Philip, Lizzie insisted on a private celebration of their own involving chandeliers, a leather rope, and a very large polished oak table. Clutching her bouquet between her teeth and sporting a black outfit designed by Cecil B. DeMille, she swung from the lights, leaving a trail of confetti behind her. Philip's vision of instructing a shy young girl in the arts of intimacy were shattered as he watched her firm round rump twirl through the air covered in little more than black lace.

He had been warned by the nanny about "our Lizzie and her secret ways," but nothing could prepare him for what he saw . . .

Or the pleasure it would give him.

Philip soon learnt to expect the unexpected from his wife. He had a trampoline installed in his bedroom, devised a network of tightropes from his den to her bedroom, and regularly cleaned out the fireplaces for Lizzie and her fire stick juggling. With just one ring of a bell, he could have her bouncing, swinging, or balancing—rose in her mouth optional. And if feeling particularly frisky, he'd give the stairs a good polish, toss his hat in the air, and shout . . .

"Where's my girl?"

Lizzie, in her best working-class persona, would appear balancing a tray of teacakes on her head.

"Afternoon tea, sir?" she'd say.

Philip always said yes.

And when Philip was feeling oppressed with his duties, Lizzie, a woman of surprising intuition, would grab a top hat, slip into her fishnets, and backflip across the hall with one of the corgis.

The servants learnt to run for cover as Philip, clutching his Polaroid, snapped away.

One picture of Lizzie's round rear sailing through the air was enough to cheer up any dreary day, and Phil had a collection of them—the most recent living in his pocket, making any tedious ceremony a breeze to sit through.

Of course, Phil knew all about Jimmie Black; Lizzie had told him, spread out on the oak table like a Renaissance princess glowing with pleasure.

"It's all about entrances and exits." She sighed. "Jimmie taught me that."

Phil told Lizzie her entrance was the best-kept secret he had ever seen. A secret Nanny kept from Lizzie's mother until the day Nanny left for the Sunset Retirement Home.

The Burning Question

For years, Lizzie's antics had gone unnoticed by her mother, a round-faced, cheery-looking woman whose permanent smile and tilt of her head gave folks the idea she was deaf. Gran was, for the most part, a kindly woman who liked to see people happy.

But she did have her limits.

At night, after a respectable amount of gin, Gran (as she was called by those close) often wandered about the palace. Passing the servants with a regal wave, she liked to breathe the evening air, make sure everyone was smiling, and perhaps sit by one of the open fires Lizzie seemed so keen on. There, alongside Nanny, she would ponder about horses, racing, and her daughter.

What gave her such a glow?

And why did Philip smirk so at the mention of leather?

She had watched her daughter sail through four pregnancies with all the ease of a rustic peasant. She had seen Phil's face, normally as glum as a winter's evening, light up at the mere mention of "I wonder what Lizzie's doing up in her room?"

Lizzie had always been a mystery to Gran, but then as Nanny said, "Aren't all children?" However, since Nanny had left, things had changed, taken on a more mysterious quality; in fact, sometimes Gran felt like she was living in an Agatha Christie novel. Nothing made sense . . .

The high crockery bill, a floor so polished you could apply your lipstick staring at it, and the new burn marks about the fireplaces every night, even in the summer—all they needed was a dead body.

She looked around the living room and counted the fire extinguishers. Somehow, fourteen seemed a little excessive. Gran's womanly intuition worked overtime, and Lizzie sprung to her mind.

Gran cornered Eddie, the most amenable of Lizzie's sons. "What are all those dark marks on the wall about? How did they get there?"

Eddie ran his fingers across his bald spot and talked of an overzealous servant lighting a fire "so big one could roast a hog on it."

Gran didn't see the joke. "But it is on the ceiling, Eddie. Was he juggling it?"

Eddie laughed a little too loudly to be natural.

Gran sat and stared at the fire, vague conversations of the past floating back to her. There were the servants' constant references to trampolines and the like in Philip's room, and Ann, Lizzie's daughter, refusing to go anywhere near the parents' floor.

"It's the rope," she said to Gran. "It appears from nowhere like a snake. And *he's* always busy polishing things, hardly notices me. May as well be one of those damnable servants," she muttered.

"Polishing?" said Gran. "What on earth is that?"

Ann shrugged her shoulders.

Gran sighed. Coping with more than one child at a time was such a trial.

"I can live with the ropes," continued Ann. "I can cope with the constant use of fire blankets. But could you speak to them about the daily slide down the banister?"

Gran closed her racing guide. "Banister? They slide down the banister?" She sighed. *I have to do something now, but what? If only Nanny were here . . .*

Gran called Lizzie into her inner sanctum, preparing for the giving of a "good dressing-down," as Nanny called it.

"Elizabeth," she said. A full name was always required for said dressing-down. "Do you really think it appropriate for the servants and the like to see you with your dress above your head and your suspenders on show?"

"I don't wear suspenders, Mother," said Lizzie.

Gran sniffed.

"Although I have been known to wear the odd G-string when Phil is a bit down."

Gran closed her eyes. "Phil?"

"Yes, Phil," said Lizzie.

"What is he, a rag-and-bone man?" said Gran.

"My hubby."

"Hubby?"

Lizzie sighed. "My husband, Philip."

"Oh, him."

Gran drained her gin, forcing herself to continue . . .

"And there's the leather, it's everywhere. I thought this family was trying to go *green*."

"That's just the prince," muttered Lizzie.

"Prince? Which one?" said Gran.

"The green one," snapped Lizzie.

Gran, now confused, drained her glass and changed tact. "Did you think I wouldn't notice?"

Lizzie said nothing.

"Do you think I'm blind?"

Lizzie looked at her shoes.

One of the servants raced by clutching a fire blanket.

Gran stopped. "Have you lit a fire?"

"No," lied Lizzie sheepishly.

Gran asked her daughter how long this *"swinging lark"* had been going on, and when Lizzie muttered something about school days, Gran nearly choked on her gin.

Lizzie looked away.

Gran's hand shook as she poured herself another drink, this time skipping the tonic.

"This is all due to that damnable Jimmie and that bloody wig he gave you. I told George to throw it away, but would he listen? Oh no, not George. 'Whatever makes Lizzie happy. Let her play her dress-up games, where's the harm?' That's what he said."

Gran glanced over the rim of her gin and looked at her daughter.

"He always spoiled you, and now look where it's got you: swinging about the palace, underwear on show for all to see. And the fires! What do you think we are made of, money? Coal does not come cheap, you know."

Lizzie continued to look at her feet.

"And where is this Jimmie now?" said Gran.

"Don't know," lied Lizzie.

"Prancing about on some bit of high wire dressed in tights, I suppose," Gran huffed.

Lizzie thought about her cousin, living in the Sunset Retirement Home, who had turned into a whisky-swilling, groin-scratching old cynic whose only memory of the past was stuck up on the walls behind his bed: photographs of a dashing young man with a glint in his eye for anything that moved and was over the legal age.

Another servant appeared lugging a fire extinguisher. He tugged at lever.

"Not here," snapped another servant, depositing a cuff across his co-worker's ear.

"Well, really," snapped Gran.

The Health and Safety Man

That night, Gran sat at the top of the great banquet table, squeezed into a pale blue evening gown with an annoying sash stretched across her chest. Her back was close to one of Lizzie's over-the-top fires, and she was sweating uncomfortably. She fanned her face with a Historic Scotland placemat while listening to the drones of a governor of some godforsaken peninsula about how "the abandonment of white trousers was the ruination of cricket."

She let out a long sigh. *Who cares?*

She stared at the chandeliers. *Is swinging the secret of a happy marriage? Does juggling brighten up a dull day of ceremonies?* She stared at her superbly chilled white wine, stunned and confused. She thought ropes were for scouts, leather for horses, and fire for sitting by. It never occurred to her that they could be used so . . . artistically.

She pushed her wine to the side. All those days wearing hats she hated and gloves that made her hands sweat, shaking hands with someone whispering in her ear.

"That's the manager of so-and-so charity, ma'am."

"Ambassador of so-and-so country, ma'am."

"The leader of so-and-so, ma'am."

While her daughter and *hubby* were having a high old time with a Polaroid and the like.

She felt let down.

Maybe she could try this so-called juggling, twirl a few oranges? After all, you're never too old, so Nanny said.

After dessert, she refused the coffee and dram with a "one felt dizzy" comment and headed down the long corridor to the kitchen.

It took her a while to find the light switch and even longer to take in what she saw. She had no idea that so many things were required for cooking. She pulled open a large dishwasher, allowing it to snap shut again. She poked at packets and ran her fingers across the shiny pots. It was nothing like *Master Chef* and *The Great British Bake-Off*.

And yet . . . intriguing.

Finally, she came across the larder. She creaked open the door, fumbled for yet another switch, and walked in. *Perhaps there is something juggle-able,* she thought, *maybe an orange or plum?*

She began to rifle through the shelves and was just in the process of sniffing a jar of cinnamon when a footman coughed from behind.

"Ma'am, the health and safety officer is here."

"Who?"

"There have been complaints about things . . ."

"And what has that to do with oranges and me?" said Gran with her sweetest smile.

"Ma'am, the palace is open to the public, and people do not want to be tripping over ropes and the like or looking at burn marks."

"This is a job for the man of the house," said Gran, clutching a bag of oranges, and with a small skid on the polished floor, she headed for her room.

Later that night . . .

Phil, after a quick scout around to see where Her Nibs (Gran) was, set up his ropes for a Lizzie swing.

Lizzie was poised and ready with a new red, white, and blue super-hero outfit she had purchased on eBay. It was not her choice, but *Phil* had just discovered Netflix and was completely obsessed with Wonder Woman.

She slid down the stairs, grabbed a rope, swung to a chandelier, and then, with a few cartwheels, ended in the kitchen. She was just contemplating a new twist on the old splits position for Phil's Polaroid when a footman coughed from behind.

"Ma'am, the health and safety officer is here."

"Who?" said Lizzie.

She turned to see a round man of five foot nothing with a clipboard and a suit too large for him. He didn't smile or bow but looked straight into Lizzie's eyes.

"There have been complaints," he said.

Lizzie looked up with her best coquettish smile, which no one ever noticed.

"And what has that to do with me? Is this not something for the man of the house?"

The health and safety officer had no time for such an argument. He was fed up working his way through the various barriers and guards explaining who he was. No one, as far as he was concerned, was above the laws of health and safety. And if members of the public were at risk of rope-tripping, then it was up to him to save them.

"Is that not you?" he said with a blank face.

"Me? I hardly think so." Lizzie looked at her hubby. "Do you know who the man of the house is?"

The health and safety officer, ignoring *Hubby's* head-shaking, continued . . .

"Ma'am, the 'man of the house' in these modern times is but a figurative term, and you, it would seem, are—is—it."

Lizzie was speechless.

"Is the palace not in your name?" he asked.

"My name?" said Lizzie.

"And the council tax?" he said.

Lizzie was now confused. She looked at Phil.

He shrugged his shoulders.

"Isn't there a servant for such things?" she finally muttered.

The health and safety officer didn't hear. He was busy looking about the kitchen, and he could tell with just a glance that something fishy was going on.

The couple watched in silence.

"What is the purpose of this harness?" he said.

Lizzie shuffled her feet.

"Err . . . holding things," said Phil, "one suspects?"

"And you do know that leather can't be sterilised?"

Lizzie fingered a chain swinging from a hook and looked at her husband. He, without a word, removed her finger.

"Sterilised?" she muttered.

"You feed the public from this kitchen, and it must be fit for that purpose, not"—he looked from one to the other—"other things."

The couple nodded.

"I mean look at this floor," snapped the health and safety man.

"What of it," Lizzie muttered feebly.

"This is not a kitchen floor polish."

"Is it not?" Phil feigned innocence.

The health and safety man glanced at Lizzie's stiletto thigh-high boots. "More for . . ."

"What?" said the couple in unison.

"Dancing?"

Lizzie staggered on her heel. Phil steadied her.

The health and safety man coughed. "Maybe the splits?"

The couple looked from one to the other . . . no one had ever spoken to them in this manner. How were they supposed to act?

"As if one would *split*—so to speak—before one's sink," said Gran, entering and clutching a gin.

Lizzie glanced at her mother; was it not her nap time? She shifted uncomfortably on her feet. She had been caught in her Wonder Woman suit, not only by a man unknown and speaking like something out of one of those soap operas Nanny liked, but by her mother. She felt like a teenager caught snogging in a car, although in truth, Phil always waited until they were in the pantry.

"Us girls," said Gran, "rarely come into the kitchen except for a banana." She winked. "Isn't that right, Lizzie?"

Lizzie looked at her mother making her way to the pantry like she did it every day.

"Us girls?" Lizzie muttered.

Gran placed a couple of bananas into a bag, followed by a ceremonial plopping of oranges, one by one, her eyes focused on the health and safety man.

He coughed and adjusted his tie as Gran, with great pomp, handed the bag to her daughter.

"Is this not what you came here for?" she said. "Some fruit before we do a bit of dressing up and nail polishing—just us girls?"

She looked at Phil.

"That's what we love, right?"

Lizzie stared at the bag of fruit and looked at her husband. "Nail polish?" muttered Phil with a dazed look.

The Tosser

It was suggested by those who ran things that a ban be placed on all acrobatic sessions in the palace except on the odd public holiday, which was completely useless to Lizzie and Philip. Public holidays were workdays for them.

"How are we to swing and wave at the same time?" said Lizzie. "I mean there are no ropes and such on the balcony, are there?"

Gran talked about lip service. "Just smile and nod," she said, "you got off lightly."

"Lightly?" muttered Phil with a downcast face. "They have confiscated my Polaroid," he huffed. He'd been given an iPhone and told to "'download'—*whatever that is*."

"Yes, imagine those photos in the hands of others," said Gran with a small burp.

"Photos of us? Who cares?" said Lizzie. "They don't even miss us on the balcony these days. Do they, *our Phil?*"

Phil said nothing; he was still brooding over his lost Polaroid.

"What with the pipe bands and horses down below, the children *and* grandchildren filling up the balcony, we may as well stay in bed. Isn't that right, our Phil?"

Phil smiled at the thought.

"Yes, well staying in bed is not what we folk do is it?" said Gran.

"And it's not like *Hello*'s knocking at our door," continued Lizzie. "We haven't been snapped in weeks."

"Speak for yourself," said Gran.

"We're old news, unless you count our Phil's swearing," giggled Lizzie.

Phil took a sip of his now-flat real ale and sighed.

How would he get through the day without his Polaroids? Mind you, with Lizzie's ropes packed away and the palace modernised with gas, there was nothing for him to *snap* anymore. *I mean a fire that came on with a switch—where's the fun in that?*

Lizzie, spurred on by Phil's downcast face, took things into her own hands. She decided to give them all a good old-fashioned bunking-off day. She stuck a *Don't knock, I am at death's door* note on her door, a *Busy fishing* on Phil's, and a *One is feeling a bit queasy* note on Gran's.

They tippy-toed into the kitchen like cartoon robbers, opened the larder like they were cracking open a safe, helped themselves to anything juggle-able, and headed for the Sunset Retirement Home.

Lizzie had a plan—a plan that included a disguise that had her in a red wig, tracksuit, and trainers and Gran in tears of laughter, until she realised she too was to wear the same.

Phil watched, for once glad he didn't have his Polaroid.

"Jimmie was always good for a laugh," Lizzie whispered. "Especially with Nanny around to rile him."

"Jimmie?" said Gran. "We're going to see Jimmie?"

"Who's Jimmie?" said Phil.

Lizzie threw him a look.

"Oh, that Jimmie," said Phil. *Could things get any worse?*

Nanny and Jimmie were sitting in the lounge room when Lizzie and her gang arrived. A comedy was playing on TV, Nanny was explaining to Jimmie why it was so funny, and Jimmie had as much interest as he did in her bunions. Old ladies in trainers were the last things he needed to see.

"Is that who I think it is?" said Nanny.

Lizzie giggled like a schoolgirl.

"Surprised you recognise me in this thing," huffed Gran.

"You bring any whisky?" shouted Jimmie.

Nanny sighed and turned the TV down. "Things aren't what they used to be," she said.

"You're telling me," snapped Gran.

Phil for once agreed with his mother-in-law.

Jimmie began to complain about his knees "playing up again," and he was in the middle of singing the praises of whisky, as opposed to "all those friggin' pills," when an ol' boy shuffled by the doorway with a Zimmer. The ol' boy stopped, stared at the new faces, then moaned about the "so-called food in this so-called establishment."

"Friggin' baby food," he shouted.

Jimmie told him to "*shut it*" and tossed an apple at him.

Gran looked at Jimmie. "You toss apples here?"

"All the time," lied Jimmie, gesturing to the bowl of fruit ignored by most.

"Knock yourself out."

Lizzie, unsure of how the *knocking out of oneself* worked, said, "How about a spot of juggling? Our gran's been practising."

Gran threw her a look.

"It'll take your mind off things," laughed Lizzie.

Phil stared at the dismal room and, for the second time that day, was glad he didn't have his Polaroid. He pulled out his iPhone and turned it in his hand. He'd been told it was ready, but for what?

Jimmie moaned about his mind being his own business, and he was just about to tell the two funny ladies and the ol' git where to *shove their business* when he spied Phil's mobile.

"You can download the cricket on that," he said.

"What? Cricket on a phone?" said Phil.

The ol' boy with the Zimmer, inspired by the idea of cricket, hurled his apple into the lounge room past Gran's head. She, inspired by her tracksuit *and trainers*, couldn't help herself and made a dive that would stop traffic.

An elderly woman sauntering past caught sight of a regal gran in a pale pink tracksuit and trainers *that flashed on each step*, lobbing a ball like a cricket pro. She stopped in her tracks.

"Mind!" shouted the nurse as the ball shot past the elderly woman's head, followed by a cartwheeling Lizzie hurling herself into a fringed lampshade to catch the ball.

"How's that?" she shouted with a spirited high kick.

A small crowd formed.

One resident, clutching his hard-boiled egg nicked from the breakfast table, was inspired.

"Cop this," he shouted. He tossed the egg into the air, then caught it with his slipper.

"If only I had my Polaroid," muttered Phil.

Jimmie, transported back to the good old days of cartwheeling and the like, turned to a mournful Phil.

"Did you get that?" said Jimmie.

Phil glared at him.

"On that." Jimmie gestured to his iPhone.

Phil turned the iPhone in his hand. "Cricket *and* photos, whatever next?"

The next week, Gran donned a caped crusader costume with a passion not seen since her Grand National days and, along with Phil and Lizzie, bunked off to the Sunset Retirement Home.

Phil watched cricket with Jimmie, and when finished, they, under the guise of *old bats have balls*, tweeted sarcastic comments about how "the abandonment of white trousers in cricket was the best thing since sliced bread," while Lizzie and Gran swung and juggled like there was no tomorrow.

Soon, dressing up and tossing things became a regular part of the day for those in the home, as the trio cheered, encouraged, and brought costumes.

And no one at any time mentioned the health and safety man, because, as one resident put it:

"Health and safety in a home only applies to the staff who work there and the public that visit. It has nothing to do with the residents."

THE STORY THAT GOT AWAY

In the beginning, there was no microchip, just a typewriter and correction fluid.

The Office

I was staring at Rodney's orange "You're Having a Laugh, It's Monday" tie when the phone rang. Rodney answered on the first ring. He dived for the phone, clutching his "Thank F It's Friday" mug, and his tie barely moved. Rodney can't bear to hear a phone ring; he has been like that ever since Barbara left.

The day Barbara left, Rodney tossed his grey tie in the bin, took down all three of her beloved grey abstracts, and pinned a sign that read "You don't have to be mad to work here, but it helps!" on the door. Now the walls are bare, with three empty grey squares, and every one of his friends that walks into the office pulls an *I'm mad, how about you?* face—and I am supposed to laugh? They are all over forty and about as zany as tea in a mug.

A bit depressing, if you ask me, but he seems happy. I have even heard him humming, and today was no different. In fact, today, Rodney was humming like a bumblebee trapped under a glass, and it was really annoying. I mean Rodney's happiness is not exactly the voice of doom, but it is usually because some horrible story is set to break, and he is about to spread it like manure on a field.

Rodney—or "Editor of the Year," as I liked to call him—runs the

Fyne News, a small newspaper in a small town, and a tragic story is really something to make a noise about.

I watched Rodney talk on the phone, oblivious to the trail of coffee he had left in mid dive. His voice was so loud it drowned out the car alarm across the road (*probably set off by some cat in hot pursuit of a takeaway wrapper*). He was definitely a changed man; freedom had opened the door to an even tackier man in love with all things that clashed. Orange ties with blue shirts, tartan trousers, and way too much facial hair to be natural . . . it seemed that the freedom of no longer living with a "style consultant" had literally gone to his head.

"I'm waiting on a phone call," Rodney shouted while holding the phone between his shoulder and ear. He mouthed "Maggie" like he did every time she phoned.

Maggie phoned most days about cats and the drive they sat on. She forgot that the drive belonged to the next-door neighbor and that her cat, Elvis, was no longer around. She complained to the police and to the home help, but no matter how many times people explained that Elvis was dead, she took no notice. Maggie continued to feed the Elvis lookalikes on the drive until one of the neighbors came out with a bucket of water. So, like every other day at noon, Maggie would again take things into her own hands and verbally abuse the only person too polite to hang up on her: her son.

Rodney put the phone back on the stand, and I began to type, hoping that the phone would ring again so I didn't have to listen to his moans about his mother and the other things that would follow. Then Rodney pulled a paper from his notepad, screwed it up into a ball, and tossed it—like a cricket bowler—at my feet.

I picked up the paper ball. "What is it this time," I said, "cat torpedoed by last night's takeaway?"

"You'll need to see her," muttered Rodney.

I knew it.

Rodney's mother had told Rodney that she had a *"wee gem of a story"* and *"could not that nice Deidre of yours come around and record it for the paper?"* Maggie's idea of a *"wee gem of a story"* was the co-op selling two tins of Go-Cat for the price of one.

I told him that I had better things to do—*which was not exactly true,*

I had nothing—and he smiled, took the paper from my hand, flicked it in the air, and, like a tennis player, hit it into the bin. The paper ball hit the wall behind it and tumbled onto the floor.

"You soothe her," he said.

"That's because I make her tea," I said. "She can't remember, and she won't remember her 'wee gem of a story' either."

I sauntered over to the paper ball in my best bored fashion and put it into the bin. I was fed up. I wanted a proper story, but Rodney wasn't listening. He, like me, knew that if I didn't go around to make tea, she'd be on the phone again. And he also, like me, knew that I had nothing better to do.

The Ned, the Jewels, and the Box

I stopped at the set of roadworks traffic lights and flashed my lights; it was going to be a long day. Maggie is not an easy woman to get away from. Once she starts on a story, you can kiss goodbye to at least a morning.

I mean that woman can talk. She may be tiny—with the legs of a sparrow and the chest of a pigeon—but my god, when she stands in a doorway gassing on, not even a laxative will move her. She will plug up her doorway for as long as her story lasts, and her stories last an eternity. This was not the first time I'd been stuck in her kitchen like a limpet on a rock with all exits closed until Maggie's story had made it to the finish line.

Once, I watched her wash out an empty tuna tin to put in the bin. *Her shower hasn't been used since the Queen's coronation, but at least the rubbish is clean, I'd thought.*

"Between you and me and the boat, they had to!" she'd said with a dramatic toss of the tin into the bin.

"What *they*? Who's *they*?" I'd said and immediately regretted it.

Maggie had tapped her nose, muttered something about a roll mop for every occasion, and then listed every occasion followed by where to get the best roll mop in the area. Two cups of tea later, I was bored out of my brain and still had no clue what a roll mop was—Maggie, when asked, had never explained.

I headed down the lane to Maggie's house. It wasn't hard to miss;

it's the only house in the street to have five black cats lounging amongst unkempt grass and a co-op trolley on its side. That trolley has been there for as long as I can remember, long before you needed a coin to use it. In the summer it has nettles growing through it, and in the winter a pile of scrunched up Carlsberg Special and Strongbow cans, courtesy of those leaving the pub after hours.

I stood at the gate and stared up at her bedroom window.

The first day I walked into the office, it felt like I was going to take on the world—I was going to be someone. I knew that just behind the next corner was the big story that would get me into *the Herald* or *the Guardian*. Five years later, I had given up waiting for the big story; instead, I spent my time picking up Rodney's messages tossed in a variety of fashions at my feet and making tea for his mother.

I was just about to go in, just about to flick the gate open, when I heard a shrill scream coming from Maggie. Maggie was quite fond of screaming, but this time it sounded different.

I charged into Maggie's house. I held my breath even before I opened the door. Her home always smelt, sometimes like fish, other times like mildew. Today, it was like an old laundry basket full of socks, a smell that would stick to my clothes like cling film.

As I entered the kitchen, I heard another scream coming from a male.

I jumped the stairs two at a time and charged into the bedroom. In the corner was a terrified-looking teenager clutching Maggie's mangled old jewellery box. He had one leg out of the window . . . which was directly above Maggie's shed.

Jesus! What had I walked into?

"In the nuts," yelled Maggie, sitting up for a better view. "Grab him."

Grab him? I'm not grabbing him. Let him jump out through the window and break his leg. I've seen what's in Maggie's jewellery box.

"Your kung fu—go on, use it," she shouted.

Two classes of karate and I'm supposed to be a Ninja Turtle risking my life for her Woolworths jewellery? I don't think so.

The young man looked down at the ground. His brain was ticking over: jump one floor down, or push past Karate Kid—me, a skinny thirty-something-year-old woman paralyzed with indecision.

Maggie reached for her glasses as the young man made his choice. "Trip him up," she shouted, "by the balls."

Physically impossible, I know, but I didn't think she'd seen any for a while.

He made for the door, and before I had time to move out of the way, he knocked me down. We rolled across the landing and down the stairs like a sack of potatoes, collecting Maggie's million and one mats along the way.

I hit my head, my arm, and my hip as I crashed about on top and then underneath a stick-thin young man with dandelion bum fluff on his chin, and as his bony hips crashed against mine, my life flashed before me. It was even sadder than Maggie's memory of a man's appendage—there wasn't a lot to see.

We landed on the floor. The unknown man scrambled to his feet and looked at me with his pale blue eyes, rubbed his backside, sniffed, and muttered an unconvincing "see you, you're for it."

I watched him vanish into the afternoon sun. An impressive feat considering his jeans hung so low. You could see not only his underpants but also his "hope is for losers" tattoo spread across the bottom of his spine.

He escaped the way he came, the door slamming behind him, leaving the faint whiff of cigarette smoke.

I hardly noticed. I was flat on my back clutching the battered jewellery box to my chest while staring at the cobwebs on the ceiling swaying from the activity. I was in shock. My life had flashed before my eyes in seconds, quicker than a roll down the stairs and more boring than Rodney's collections of ties.

I went back to the car. I had my story and a title, and I scribbled it down before I could even think. *"How Does a Fall down the Stairs Change Your Life?"*

The Story

When I told Rodney about the young man, Rodney was excited. "This could be serious," he said. "This could put *Fyne News* on the map. Tell me everything." He was standing in his Lycra cycling shorts at the time. Now a single man—and, according to his shorts, swinging freely —he'd taken to cycling to work.

"This thing is big," he said. "If we don't jump on the wagon, it's gonna go without us."

Rodney always talked like that when excited, and he was pretty excited about the robbery that had almost happened. Not much happens in Lochgilphead; it is a small town, and "big" in the *Fyne News* was anything that wasn't an ad for the paper.

"Yes, we need to get going with this one," he said, with a mild strut to the water cooler. "After all, it's not often someone gets done in Lochgilphead."

I attempted to tell him that Maggie hadn't been *done,* but rather it was she who had scared the crap out of a ned. Rodney looked at me. "How could a five-foot-nothing woman with matching bunions and a love of cats scare anyone? My mother's a sweet old lady."

What planet is he on? Maggie, sweet? Maggie may be many things, but sweet isn't one of them. And her bravery is all around Lochgilphead. She's even given a round of applause in the chemist, as well as a free blood pressure test.

But Rodney was on a roll. "We can't afford to fanny around. I need some meat for the next paper," he said with an unnecessarily hard tug at the paper cup dispenser, "and I don't mean bloody gristle."

I stared out of the window. *Rodney is a real caveman.*

"I want you to start digging," he continued. "The neighbors said they heard screaming on par with a cat being separated from its balls." He looked at me. "We could put that in. In fact, why don't you go and visit the neighbors? Maybe they have something on this ned."

Rodney skulled his water, crunched the paper cup in one hand, and kicked it across the room like a footballer. And just like a footballer, he missed the bin, completely splattering the remains of the water onto the wall behind the bin.

I guess cycling shorts don't improve one's aim on things either.

The Real Story

Rodney's moods go around like a revolving door. If you don't get off at the right point, you are outside again. He can promise the earth, your name on the front page, and a story that has people crying out for more. But in the end, what you end up with is a scrunched-up paper tossed at your feet and your story sliced and diced with his name at the bottom.

He always blamed Barbara. "She's the boss," he'd say, pulling a face. "What she says goes." And nothing has changed. In the few months since Barbara and her paintings have disappeared, my stories have still landed on the floor by my feet, and his name is still the only one that appears in the *Fyne News*.

Barbara was now designing covers for *Fabulous You*, a magazine for women. One cold Monday morning, she dropped Rodney off at the office, told him she was going for bacon rolls, and never returned. Rodney went through many phases of loss: he drank too much, lost weight, and wrote love notes to her which, in the end, turned into abusive rants. And for a while, I felt sorry for him.

Myself, I have always gone for a more dignified split—even if it was only once. I didn't even keep the engagement ring. Derek, my ex, said he understood, that we would remain friends, and he warned me against Rodney. "You'll never get a story in that paper," he said. "No one does but Rodney."

Funnily enough, Barbara often said the same thing, along with the odd comment about Derek being as tight as the *Fyne News*'s budget. "No decent man takes back a ring," she said. "Even Rodney wouldn't do that." But then, as Maggie pointed out, Rodney never given Barbara one in the first place.

I decided that Saturday morning was the best time to drop in and see Maggie's neighbors. There was a coffee morning in one of the churches, and Maggie loves her coffee mornings. Maggie loves any food that has the word *cake* at the end: fishcakes, cream cakes, potato cakes. I knew she wouldn't be around wanting me to make her tea.

I didn't fancy going back to her place. The last thing I wanted to do was recreate the memory of a fall down the stairs wrapped in the arms of a ned or have another set of clothes to wash the sock smell out of.

The fall down the stairs was still haunting me. I felt like I had wasted five years in that newspaper believing Rodney's promises, and I wanted to change. I wanted to stop running around for Rodney and create work with my name on it.

I had lived in Lochgilphead all my life. I knew the best places to camp, the best forestry walks, and I knew enough people to make walking down the main street a slow process of "hiyas." All my friends were settled, some with children, most with partners, and some, like Derek, were living miles away, while I was still living in a caravan waiting for Rodney to deliver what he had promised from the beginning: my name at the bottom of my story.

"Your stories will be in the paper soon," he said. "We just need to refine you a bit."

I parked the car at the co-op, checked my face in the mirror, smeared a little Chapstick on my lips, and headed out.

The pipe band had filled the entrance of the co-op, making it impossible to pass without a coin bucket pushed under your nose. They were playing *Knees Up Mother Brown* to an empty car park, and it was going down like yesterday's takeaway. I looked out onto the main street and there she was on her black-and-gold scooter, oblivious to anyone else on the pavement.

The scooter—or Pricilla, as she likes to call it—is as much a part of Maggie as her phone calls to the *Fyne News*. It has a horn which toots "Viva Las Vegas" and thick wheels for the bumpy footpath. Pricilla is a supersized buggy and, much to Maggie's delight, takes up nearly the whole of the footpath. When Maggie drives her buggy, everyone has to jump out of her way.

Maggie saw me and waved.

"When is a kipper not a kipper?" she shouted with a laugh as the pipe band started up a rousing *Flower of Scotland,* drowning out any possibility of a reply. If there was a story there, then I suspected it had nothing to do with the ned and more to do with Maggie. Any woman that could hold a pavement to ransom must have some sort of history.

Fish Paste—Not for the Faint-Hearted

I watched Maggie pour hot water into her Captain Pugwash teapot, toss a used teabag in it, put the lid back, and turn it anticlockwise three times. Then she took some fish paste sandwiches out of the oven and placed them on a paper towel. *Apparently, paper towels not only save on washing up but can be used again if given a good shake.* I stared at the edges of the sandwiches curling towards the ceiling and quickly scanned the kitchen for anywhere I could dump her tea and bread when she wasn't looking.

I had sat here many times with Maggie and still knew nothing about her. I had mended her kitchen shelves and dripping taps. I had fed so many of her sandwiches to the birds that they now wait outside her house until I come out. I had even, on several occasions, sat outside with her and counted the many black cats that now hung about her garden. I had asked Maggie about them, but getting her to focus was not always easy, especially when one of the cats could be heard thudding an entrance from the kitchen window.

"Elvis needs feeding," she often muttered. *The original Elvis was buried in the empty cabbage patch, along with Elvis Two, Elvis Three, and a cat called Puss,* but to Maggie, any of the army of cats that paraded downstairs was Elvis. She fed them all, and it was always fish—fish of the highest-smelling variety—and the smell sank into my fingers and my clothes.

I looked out of the kitchen window and saw the shed door flapping in the wind; apparently, the ned had tried the shed too. But thanks to a robust overgrowth of nettles and brambles, he didn't get very far except to pull the window open an inch and wrench the door off one of its hinges. Maggie was happy for me to mend it, and I was happy to get away from her tea and sandwiches.

I spent the morning battling the nettles around the entrance of the shed. I finally made my way through the door, skidded on a pool of oil, and lost my balance. I grabbed hold of the closest thing to hand, a rake, which in turn knocked over a stack of tins along with the shelf that held said tins.

Maggie shouted something along the lines of "mind my cabbages and the like," which I chose to ignore, preferring instead to swear like a drunk at closing time as my head scraped against the brick wall and took some "green sticky stuff" along with it.

It took me a whole afternoon to sort, and I was just about to throw the tins into some dark hole when I heard a rattle and wondered . . .

There, in her tins, was Maggie's past life, a life I had never imagined her living, on a Loch Fyne I never knew: photographs of an athletic-looking redhead—a woman who "turned heads" and was nothing like the old woman capable of scaring the balls off a ned.

I searched through the photos and came across the most impressive one: her holding up the largest salmon I had ever seen. I stared at her tiny frame dwarfed by the large fish. She must have been twenty, max, and there was not a single cat in sight.

I heard feet making a sucking, squelching noise in the mud outside. I jumped to my feet and turned; Maggie was standing in the doorway. "He was looking for that," she said, "just like his grandfather. That bastard led me up more garden paths than a botanical garden."

Normally, when she starts talking like that, it's time to put the brandy away and get out the fireguard. But this time, I wondered. I stared at her; she had her Captain Pugwash teapot in one hand and the sandwiches in the other. I watched her pour the tea over the cabbage patch and toss the sandwiches to the birds. "Fish paste is good for the birds," she said, chuckling.

And I thought they were for me.

That afternoon, I went back to the office and started to write. The office was empty, thanks to a bout of "man flu." Rodney, apart from me, was the only one not at home nursing a cold. Rodney had taken to sleeping with half an onion by his pillow, thanks to the *Fyne New's* regular Nature's Cure article. And not only did it cure his rhinitis, it also played a major part in the *split*—so he said.

Personally, I like to think that a woman as intelligent as Rodney's ex had left her husband of twenty years for more than just a whiff of onion.

I spent all afternoon in the office, inspired. I wrote like there was no tomorrow. I wrote like there was a jet up my proverbial, like I couldn't breathe if I didn't get the words out.

Maggie's stories brought back memories of a time when I was little and life was good. When I went fishing with my father, cooked what we caught over a campfire, and told him stories, a million miles away from the flashback at the bottom of Maggie's stairs.

Maggie was a great fisherwoman. She had landed the largest salmon in Scotland. She had wrestled it from the water and broke all the records. And I had spent the better part of an afternoon listening to her over brandy and fruitcake.

"I used to go out every morning," said Maggie. "The times we spent out on the lochs, watching the sun rise and set." She sighed. "He taught me every knot you could tie."

Maggie bent down and stroked an Elvis lookalike. Her face softened as the cat rubbed against her knees. "There is nothing like the spray of the sea on your face and the thrill of riding a wave," she said.

It felt great to be inspired, to feel the rich tapestry of creativity flowing through my veins again. And I was firing on every single creative cylinder you could name until Rodney walked in.

He closed the door with an *I've had one hell of a day and need a tea* slam. He flicked on the kettle and poured at least three teaspoons of sugar into his mug. All afternoon, I had been writing a story to be proud of. I could feel it in my waters, and now, with a slam of an office door, the flow had stopped.

Rodney squeezed his teabag and tossed it at the bin. It hit the wall behind the bin before landing on the floor, adding a darker tone to the watermarks already dried on the wall. I picked up the bag and put it in the bin. What was wrong with Rodney? He used to have the aim of Beckham. I'd seen him toss a paperclip into the drawer from outside the office while rolling a cigarette and talking on the phone.

At first, Rodney wanted nothing to do with my story. He was so incensed that he nearly screwed it up until I grabbed it off him. "So what the hell am *I* going to do for a story now?" he said. "I was banking on the ned."

Rodney's trim was not great, and I had no idea why, but I continued to talk about his mother. It was such a great story, and I knew once he heard it, he would see its greatness too. I told Rodney about how Maggie had asked me back into the kitchen, how she talked through all her photos about her life when she was young.

"Maybe next week," he finally muttered. "I was really looking for something punchier."

I told him that the ned was not actually a ned but the grandson of Maggie's old fishing partner.

"My mother fished?"

"Did she fish? She broke every record going. Her face was even on the *Scottish Angler* magazine," I said.

"I hate fishing," muttered Rodney.

"The boy wanted the photos, nothing sinister," I said.

"What?"

"Of Scotland's largest salmon. There is a picture of your mum—she caught it. And she told him it was in the jewellery box, enticed him upstairs, and started screaming."

"Typical."

"She wanted revenge."

"Revenge for what, stealing her bait?"

"Because," I said dramatically, "the grandfather had promised her the moon and then left her with nothing."

"Oh, I can relate to that."

"Your mother had caught the biggest salmon ever in Scotland, and the grandfather took all the credit. He had that salmon stuffed and mounted in his hotel." I told Rodney how Maggie was disgusted. "'What a waste,' she said. 'I mean that could have fed the cats for weeks and even months.'"

Rodney chuckled. "Sounds like her."

Rodney was warming to the idea, I could tell, so I continued. "Maggie said, 'He wasn't getting my photos, and neither was anyone else in that damn family.' And then do you know what else she said?"

Rodney waited.

"'If people think you're mad, they'll leave you alone, and there is nothing like the flash from the old yin to scare a young 'un away. That boy will go home thinking I am nuts. He'll never come back here again, and that bastard will never get his hand on my photographs.'"

Rodney started to laugh. "She flashed at the ned? Doesn't surprise me. She terrorised my friends when I was young and scared my father off. She even reduced a mechanic to tears—over an MOT."

Rodney looked at the title of my story, *"Famous Last Catch."* "Catchy title," he muttered. He picked it up, flicked through the pages, and began to read. He even chuckled at some points. "You make her sound human," he said, and for the first time ever, he placed my story back on my desk rather than in the bin and offered me a coffee.

Rodney pulled two Nescafé sachets and a packet of Twix from his drawer. He pulled a seat up beside me and started to talk about the hell of a week he'd had. The paper, apparently, was losing money or, to quote Rodney, "dying on its knees." *I had no idea.*

"I thought I could pull some funds from somewhere," he said. "But it's all going, and as if that was not bad enough, she's coming for the paintings."

"I see."

"She's coming back for her rubbish art, and I, for the life of me, can't remember where I stored them."

A few days later, Barbara walked into the office. She looked amazingly successful—and chatty, which was a surprise, as she hardly talked to me when she worked on the paper. She was always in and out trying to land advertisements, stressing and arguing with Rodney about money.

Rodney had remembered where he had stashed the paintings and had them in the office ready for her to pick up. He had resigned himself to the fact that the newspaper was closing and begun to make plans for training for the next triathlon. I supposed in brand-new cycling shorts.

"He should have left with me," said Barbara. "Now the paper has been taken over, and he's got nothing, not even a job."

Rodney didn't seem to mind. He even talked about sorting out his mother's garden, starting with "that graveyard of a cabbage patch."

Barbara eyed the Nescafé sachets in the bin and smiled. "He finally liked one of your stories," she said. *Apparently, the Nescafé sachets only come out for special occasions.* "And a Twix bar as well; must be worth a read."

Barbara picked up the story . . .

It was last Saturday afternoon when it all "kicked off." Maggie was in her bed taking one of her catnaps when a rumble woke her. She looked up to find a young man helping himself to her "ornaments" and acted on impulse.

"Any port in a storm?" she shouted while flashing her wares.

The young man had taken one look and panicked. He had been in a few "jobs," seen a few things, but nothing had prepared him for the sight of Maggie and her Crimplene underwear.

Barbara was impressed. She never did like Rodney's mother. But when she got to the section about Maggie reminiscing in her kitchen, her face softened.

Maggie supped on her brandy, her round face peering into the past as she looked at her photos.

"I taught him all he knows," she said. "And at first, he was grateful. He even helped me design a fly like no other—the "Now or Never"—and it floated across the waves, spinning like a diamond hanging from an earlobe.

Barbara, like Rodney, had no idea that Maggie liked to fish. She had no idea about the giant salmon, now stuffed and framed in a rundown hotel miles from anywhere. She continued to read about the shed, the photographs, and, of course, the catch itself . . .

Maggie rode the waves like she was part of the sea, chasing the great salmon like the Moby Dick of Argyll. She tossed the Now or Never into the water, dancing it on the surface, tantalising the salmon. It was her greatest moment and her final downfall.

When Barbara had finished, she made a copy and asked me if there were more.

"Of course," I told her. "There are plenty."

A Few Months Later

Fabulous You loved my story, and soon I was writing stories for them every month, and when *Fyne News* was sold to a bigger company, they too asked me to stay on, but I refused. I didn't want the next five years to feel like the last. Besides, *Fabulous You* had given me a column; Barbara had convinced them my style would add "freshness" to the magazine.

She said, "Anyone who could recant stories from a woman like Maggie, who could make fishing not only readable but almost sexy, should be given a chance." She also said that if *Fabulous You* didn't pick me up, someone else would.

Fabulous You agreed, and Deidre McPherson, the writer, was born. I had finally outgrown my hometown and, within months, built a following that would keep me going for years. And Rodney? He opened up a bait and tackle shop, won three triathlons, and joined the local football team (his aim, now back to its former glory, before the collapse of the *Fyne News*). He restored Maggie's garden, rebuilt the shed, and copied her photos onto his laptop.

I even wrote a story about him, about cycling and recycling. Rodney, stylishly coordinated in a silver tracksuit and dark trainers, agreed to pose for a picture. He happily stood in his shop posing by his latest multi-geared, super-lightweight bike. And this time, there was not an orange tie or a pair of cycling shorts in sight—just a photo of a young Maggie holding up her salmon hanging on the wall behind his head.

MAVIS AND ME "DO" HALF-LIFE

One woman's art is another's "what the fuck?"

Mavis and I walked into the Argyll for a quick one; I had my walking shoes and dad's jacket on for warmth, while Mavis had opted for leather, lipstick, and flowery wellies.

Mavis posed by the bar; she had two tickets for the *Half-Life* show and a novel's worth of opinions about it. Mavis likes to think she's arty. Me? I'm more a Rubens fan: lots of fat women, safely framed and hanging in a warm room with coffee and a toilet nearby.

For a woman of a certain age, that's comfort.

"You headin' for the Antarctic?" said Malcolm, the barman.

Malcolm is sort of guy who thinks culture is anything written in French and Gaelic is what the French cook mushrooms in; he wouldn't know art if it jumped up and ripped his nails out one by one, and he wasn't impressed when we told him about *Half-Life*.

"What's that when it's at home?" he said.

"It's outdoor art," said Mavis, "something to do with bones and cremation, and we've been invited."

Half-Life is a play held in the middle of a forest, and the only way to get there is on a double-decker bus. Mavis and I, along with the rest of the audience, waited for the bus on the Lochgilphead green in a tent with fairy lights and candles. Mavis liked the tent (or "marquee," as she liked to call it). She said it put her in mind of an elegant wedding, and the only thing "lacking," as far as she was concerned, was the "lubrication of alcohol, preferably gin." To be honest, if it wasn't for the free ticket, I wouldn't have bothered; *Coronation Street* was at a crucial stage, and it was only Mavis's offer to wear her flowery wellies that swung it for me. Mavis doesn't 'do' wellies.

We sat at the top of the bus right at the back and for the first time, through a small film of mist, saw Lochgilphead from above. It was like being back at school again, without the cigarettes. Even the co-op looked impressive.

Mavis, who wanted to get into the spirit of *Half-Life*, had insisted on us visiting the two forts Dunadd and Druim an Duin. We squelched our way through the mud to reach Druim an Duin and then walked to the top of Dunadd. Mavis stood at the top of the hill like someone out of a Victorian drama as the wind and the sound effects mingled together like something out of a film.

"I feel like the past has touched me," she said, staring across the moss.

"We used to sneak up here, remember? A bit of rum, some Coke, and, if we were lucky, one of the McLean boys . . . we made own background noises back then."

"Hmm, the circle of life," said Mavis, looking pensive. "And it all starts with just a few sound effects."

Mavis and I sat through the show. It was long enough to make us glad we'd brought our cushions, atmospheric enough to make us stay awake and wonder what was happening next, and different enough to make me glad I had taped *Coronation Street* rather than watched it.

"That was absolutely fantastic," said a woman from behind.

"Aye well, it's amazing what they can do with a few trees, a bit of lighting, and some harnesses," said her partner.

"And how those two trapeze artists hung upside down for so long without getting dizzy," continued the woman. "That was amazing."

"I didn't understand it," says Mavis.

"You're not meant to understand it," said the woman. "It's the experience. Watching the bats . . . thinking about death and bones and things . . ."

"For twenty quid, I would want to understand," said Mavis.

"It's the lights, the atmosphere, the ambiance . . ."

"I can get that with a couple of tea lights and a gin," snapped Mavis.

"Still, it makes you think," I said.

"What, about a drink at the Argyll?"

"No," I said, "about the circle of life, the coming and goings . . . are we dead when we stop breathing, where do we go when we are dead, that sort of thing."

Mavis looked at me as if she had seen me for the first time.

"So," said Malcolm, "how was the *Half-Life* then? You see any cremations?"

"No," said Mavis, lifting her tray of drinks. "Let's just say it was nothing like I expected."

Mavis took the tray back to the table; a few from the bus had joined us for a drink.

"It was amazing," said one of the women at the top of her voice.

"Brilliant," said her partner.

"What were you expecting?" I said to Mavis.

"I don't know," said Mavis. "Something Neolithic I suppose."

I don't know what I had expected either, but as I looked at the television screen on the wall and then at the fresh-faced people around me arguing over the merits and meaning of *Half-Life*, it suddenly dawned on me that *Coronation Street* had not even entered my head once, during the whole evening.

HALLOWEEN AND CHRISTMAS LIGHTS

Chipping away at the granite of life is what gets many up in the morning. Others use jokes.

It was Halloween, and I (keeping with the Halloween theme) was merrily teaching gothic tilts to my flock of three belly dancers.

Sandra, Karin, and Margaret had been loyal students for months, which I suspect had as much to do with my comic stories of Rodger, a man I dreaded coming home to, as my shimmies.

Rodger, due to the sort of childhood many found hard to believe, refused to celebrate anything. He was brought up in an old folks' home ran by his mother. His childhood memories of Christmas, Halloween, Easter, and birthdays were of him entertaining the elderly dressed as a dog.

Not alone, but accompanied by a mother who wanted to be a comedian and a father with a yen for performing famous female sixties singers' catalogs (Barbara Streisand and Shirley Basse being his favourite). Rodger's father had a thing for women with rigid hairstyles.

Where the dog came into it, I had no idea; Rodger never got far enough to explain. It took him several whiskies to mention his mother, several more the dogs' outfit, and then he usually passed out.

My class loved my Rodger jokes, although they never said anything. I could tell . . . I mean they never told me to shut up. Sometimes they even laughed.

Tonight, however, Margaret seemed to be somewhere else, despite being a dedicated Sting fan. She was on a rant, a rant that was as unstoppable as the tide and loud enough to drown out *"Desert Rose"*—her favourite Sting song—playing full volume.

"Halloween, who wants it?" she shouted. "Demented mothers mouthing obscenities at unyielding turnips while knocking up costumes with egg boxes and crêpe paper. You can stuff it!"

I stopped.

Margaret loved Halloween, especially the costumes. No egg box was safe in her hands, and as for turnips, I've seen her whip up a face in the time it took Sting to sing "Roxanne." She was the enthusiastic one, the believer of all worth celebrating. If she lost faith . . .

I threw myself into "Rodger antidote" mode.

"Thanks to an unfortunate incident with a dog costume and a female impersonator, Rodger has a thing about Halloween." I said. "The mere mention of apple bobbing has him running to the shed."

The girls twirled—Margaret without a laugh.

"And don't get me started on Christmas," I said.

Silence.

Sandra frowned, Karin rolled her eyes, while Margaret threw me a dark look and swore under her breath.

"I hate Halloween!" she said.

"So does my Rodger," I said. "Trick-or-treating fair puts a droop in his swinging. One knock-knock joke and he is as limp as a dunked rich tea biscuit."

"All that chipping-away-at-a-turnip malarkey," said Margaret.

"What about a pumpkin?" said Sandra with a look at me.

"Pumpkins are for wimps," she snapped. "Anyone can sculpt a pumpkin, but a turnip takes skill, precision."

"And the arms of an ox," I laughed.

"There was me, gluing eggs boxes to tights," said Margaret, "with children more interested in their mobiles than tea lights. And where was my hubby?"

I was about to say, "Hiding under the sink?" but I caught a look from Sandra and gave it a miss.

"Glued to *Strictly Come Dancing*, ogling over Felicity Kendal's ability to do the splits."

"Felicity Kendal's still alive?" muttered Karin.

"I had just spent the last few hours helping *his* kids create the turnip of the century," said Margaret, "and there he was drooling over some blonde with good lighting."

She huffed mid shimmy.

"Three hours it took"—she looked about the room—"three hours . . . along with enough McDonald's promises to break a bank."

The room was quiet. A toilet flushed from down the hall.

"It's not easy keeping kids happy. In my day, an empty cornflakes box, a handful of nuts, and a satsuma were enough. Now it's apps and iPads . . . and more snacks to choose from than that Felicity probably has in hair dye. The least *he* could have done was appreciate my work . . ."

She tossed her scarf on the floor.

"Like to see bleeding Felicity make a turnip work."

Karin turned to Sandra. "You sure she's not dead?"

Sandra mouthed a "no."

"There I was, turnip in one hand and paring knife in the other, and do you know what he said? 'She's the same age as you, isn't she?'"

"She's older," I muttered.

"I know that," snapped Margaret.

The music stopped.

Margaret prided herself in her belly dancing hips. The power of her shimmy was legendary. It was like an unbalanced washing machine on full spin, and, up till Felicity Kendal's splits, it had her hubby hypnotised.

"The only thing keeping my hubby and that knife apart was his dad," she snapped.

"Jesus," muttered Karin.

"He was in the room too. Going on about *The Good Life* and Felicity's Rear of the Year award."

"She does look good for her age," muttered Sandra.

Margaret glared at Sheryl.

"I may not be able to do the spits," said Margaret. "But I can shimmy my clothes off with no hands—even the underwire."

"Bit too much information," muttered Karin.

I tried to continue with the class, but it was pointless; Margaret had spoilt the ambience. Even the tantric laments of Sting couldn't budge her dark mood. In fact, Sting was beginning to grate.

Sandra told Margaret to "give the guy a break, we all have our fantasies." She gestured to the janitor in the hall. "He'd give his tool bag and more for a night with Karin."

Karin jumped. "What?"

"Why do you think he's always popping in? Bleeding the radiators? They don't even work; central heating was put in years ago."

Karin's tight bun almost flickered with embarrassment.

"He just wants to catch a glimpse of you," said Sheryl. "See you shimmy."

Karin looked at me. I shrugged my shoulders as the door burst open. The janitor entered with a nonchalant whistle, dumped his tool bag by a heater, and squatted with a grunt.

We watched in silence as he pulled out a wrench and tried to twist the un-twistable.

"Fantasy?" said Margaret. "Well, if Felicity Kendal and her yoga legs is my husband's fantasy, then do you know what *my* fantasy is?"

No one asked.

"Choking said hubby with my belly dancing fucking thighs," said Margaret stoically, circling her hips.

"Bit dramatic," muttered the janitor.

I, clutching two fish suppers, headed home.

Every year it was the same thing: Rodger moaning and me fed up. For twenty years I had missed out on trick-or-treating, Christmas trees, and Easter eggs, not to mention birthdays. I was lucky if he made me a coffee let alone wished me a happy birthday.

I wanted to dress up, decorate the house, welcome folk in. I wanted to hear their jokes and hand out gooey food, not sit with the lights out and him in the shed shouting, "Turn the TV down, there's someone at the door."

Living with Rodger was like living with a psychotic teenager.

I arrived home to see Rodger looking comfortable by the fire, munching on an apple.

I was surprised; the only thing Rodger usually did with an apple was toss it at the next-door neighbor's cat.

He bit into the flesh. "How was the class?"

"Interesting," I said.

"Margaret, was she there?"

"Yes, and spitting chips," I said. "Something to do with Felicity Kendal and turnips—it was hard to make out. I think she's gone off Halloween."

Rodger stretched his legs in front of the fire and took another chomp.

"Understandable."

I looked at Rodger, a man who took smug to a new level.

"What do you mean?"

"It's a horrendous time, all those pumpkins and turnips. Look at what I went through."

"You don't look too cut up," I said.

"I met Margaret's husband."

He looked at me.

I watched him polish his apple off with precision.

"Apparently, I am the reason they come to your class. I'm the butt of all your stupid jokes."

He tossed the core into the fire.

"My childhood was as painful as standing on an upturned plug with no shoes . . ."

I stared at the fire. *That was one of my jokes.*

" . . . just as you stubbed your ingrown toenail."

So was that.

"You've turned my pain into a comedy routine. I mean it was bad enough growing up with a mother trying to be funny, but you—my wife?"

I looked at him.

"You've made fun of me," he said.

"Only behind your back," I muttered.

I knew Rodger didn't have much of a sense of humor, but when he moved out the next day, I realised just how little.

It seems that nothing I said amused him—for years.

I tried to convince him to stay. I told him I'd tone down the jokes, cut him out of them altogether.

"Impossible," he snapped, pulling suitcases from the loft.

"Twenty years," I said to him. "How can you throw it all away, just like that?"

He said I had thrown it away, that I was the one callous enough to use his pain for my gain.

"Hardly a gain," I said. "Three pupils and one of them is waning." *Margaret was talking of line dancing.*

Rodger was unmoved.

I watched him fill a case with socks and shove a bottle of after-shave on the top, followed by *my* hairbrush.

"There always someone's butt in a joke," I said. "What is humor but jeering, sarcasm, taking the piss? When someone falls down, do you not laugh, chuckle when they hit their head?"

"No, I usually help," hissed Rodger, ramming his Y-fronts into a co-op bag. He grabbed his bags and clattered down the stairs.

I followed.

"But you like Ricky Gervais, Monty Python, Billy Connolly . . ."

He stopped at the front door and glared at me. "But they are funny, and they're *men*. Men make the jokes, woman laugh."

I was about to make a quip about men compensating for penis sizes and then decided it was probably best not to. Instead, I followed him to the shed and watched as he cleared it, filling his car with tools he never used.

"I'm moving back into the old folks' home to think," he said.

"Think? There? With all that incontinence?" I blurted.

"See what I mean? Nothing is sacred to you. It's all a big fucking game."

I looked at him. I had no idea what he was talking about. All I knew was that I now had a spare wardrobe, an empty shed, and no tools to fix a leak if there was one.

"Maybe I'll dress up as Santa," said Rodger, tossing the last of his bags into the back of the car.

"Santa?" I muttered as Rodger, with a fair amount of wheel spinning, disappeared around the corner.

I couldn't believe it. I thought that my life was mapped out in front of me, that Rodger would annoy me to my grave. I never thought he'd leave. That I would be standing at the front door dreading going in, future unknown.

I was in shock.

Hurt and upset, I dragged myself to the next belly dancing class. There was not a joke left inside of me.

Sandra and Karin arrived early. As I set up the music, they waited for a joke, and when none came, they began to talk of Margaret, who had apparently gone home to verbally bash her husband.

"Turns out she completely misunderstood him," said Sandra.

"She's good at that," said Karin. "Never quite gets a compliment."

Sheryl asked me what was wrong. I told her I felt like an empty takeaway box crumpled by a full rubbish bin.

She looked at me like I was speaking Swahili.

"He's left her," said Margaret, arriving with a soft look.

Karin stopped, scarf about her hips. "I'm sorry," she muttered.

Sandra, with a stoical knotting of her scarf, switched off the music and looked at me. "You can trick-or-treat to your heart's content now."

"I thought he liked my sense of humor," I muttered.

The girls threw me a *really* look.

"Well, he never said he didn't," I said. "I just assumed he wasn't the laughing sort."

"Not laughing is a pretty good sign that a joke is not funny," said Sandra.

I muttered an "oh."

"Just think of the Christmas trees, all the fairy lights you can fill your home with now," said Karin.

"You can go crazy," said Margaret.

"I guess," I muttered.

"A door has opened, not closed," said Karin.

I looked at her. "Door?"

"You don't have to crack jokes to hide what hurts anymore."

I never thought of that. I nodded.

"And we can learn to dance without listening to your stupid Rodger jokes," said Sandra.

BOUDICCA AND MAVIS

The riding of a horse does not always require a saddle.

The Sleeping Dog

It was a horse, but not as you'd know it.

I was promised a stallion, large, white, and decorated like a Celtic Christmas tree. And I pictured me, on that horse, with a war cry to silence a town.

Mavis said I was nuts.

I had been asked to play Boudicca for the Lochgilphead lantern festival. And I had been promised a horse that people would never forget.

Nobody mentioned anything about papier mâché . . .

The theme was "Celtic heroes," and I'd been chosen to play Boudicca—a role a woman like me could relate to. I had been promised a lot (except for a costume and a fee) and was looking forward to the big adventure, despite Mavis's warnings.

I was, after all, the main attraction.

Mavis says I would "do anything for attention," that I'm "so driven for an audience" that I would sell not only my soul but my best friend, my matching mugs, and the secret recipe for long-life, lighter-than-air mayonnaise.

Of course, I disagreed with her. I have no idea how to make mayonnaise.

"Attention is not all it's cracked up to be," she said, reminding me of the Christmas do.

"That was different," I said. "That was Rodger's idea. This time, I am surprising him, and he won't know what's hit him."

Mavis was skeptical.

"Just wait till he sees me astride that horse," I said. "He won't be able to take his eyes off me. And it'll be a great promotion for my dance classes. Women will look at me and see the wild woman within; in fact, when the paper interviews me, that's what I am going to say."

"They didn't interview you last time, did they?" said Mavis. "They didn't even ask you what you thought. They just printed a story that made you look . . . well . . . not in the best of lights, and it didn't help your classes either."

"No one starts a new class at Christmastime," I said with little conviction.

Last Christmas, Rodger asked me to perform for the old folks' do. When I say "asked," I mean Rodger came home one evening after a few in the Argyll and told me that the Argyll had been left in the lurch —a lurch that I could fill.

I should have known better.

Rodger has an imaginative, make-do approach to things, especially anything remotely DIY. And his pledge of "props to die for" should have warned me. I mean Rodger's idea of a dancer's prop is a solar-powered torch for lighting along with an upload on his mobile: not the easiest thing to belly dance to.

Rodger sat me on a hospital trolley under a giant papier mâché Christmas pudding.

"Jump out like a strippergram," he said, "give 'em some of your Middle Eastern promise."

My entrance was as far from Middle Eastern promise as a Catholic priest. The hospital trolley squeaked like a trapped mouse, the papier mâché clung to me like cling film, and my audience was as lukewarm as yesterday's fry-up.

The local paper made a meal of it. They published a piece cryptically called "A Bite at First Sight," and it took three of Mavis's finest whiskies for me to read . . .

It was the old folks' Christmas do, and the Argyll had promised something special.

They promised melt-in-your-mouth turkey, trimmings you'd talk about for days, and a pudding that was so much more than dried fruit.

"I don't just give 'em gravy and trimmings," said Shifty, the manager, "I give 'em entertainment they will dine out on for years."

The music started as Rodger pulled a large plum pudding into the bar. Ethel, a vocal woman who many claimed had fought in the Vietnam War, stared in silence. We all did, as the music was like nothing heard before. It was music that made a cat's howl sound like a harp, the scream of a baby like a lullaby, and a nail scraping down a blackboard like a delightful twinkle of wind chimes. It was so bad that Bingo, Shifty's dog, began to howl like a wolf at a full moon.

Rodger positioned the plum pudding in the middle of the floor and poured brandy over it. The fumes were strong, and a few coughed, while others muttered at the wastage. Then, Rodger lit the pudding and smoke filled the room. There were gasps from us all and a few shouts of "oh, for God's sakes" at the rear.

We heard a scream followed by some feeble punching; someone yelled for a fireman, another switched off the lights, while most grabbed their drinks and headed for the door. But Ethel knew what to do—as she said, she "hadn't trekked across half of Vietnam with a backpack the size of a shopping bag for nothing"—and with a pint of Tartan Special and a can of Coke, she surprised us all.

Nefertiti, like a mole through a tunnel, pushed her hand through soggy paper and waved a veil . . .

"I am Nefertiti, watch me roar!"

Bingo, a bite-sized dachshund, jumped on the trolley and made a dive for the veil, and the pudding collapsed.

Nefertiti, however, was not to be stopped; armed with her sequined padded bra and Boots spray-on tan, she meant business, and a pint-size dog was not going to put her off. Within seconds, she was off the trolley and into the splits, causing a few in the audience to wince. Then, before anyone could bark "werewolf," she pulled

Turkish delights from a variety of crevices and lobbed them at Bingo.

But Bingo is a dog with a savory rather than sweet tooth, a dog with a talent for high jumping. Nefertiti's Dance of the Seven Veils was no match for Bingo, who made a beeline for her bra.

It was a scene remembered by some and talked about by a few, and it lifted Bingo into the limelight, forever known as "the dog that bites where few dare."

The Beard

Clutching my makeshift costume of itchy tartan, I pulled up a chair at the make-up station. I was sitting in the community center, staring at the young face of an organiser (anyone in an orange jacket) as she prepared to paint my face.

"Look, a beard would really work," she said, dabbing a brush into a pot of blue face paint.

"But she didn't have a beard," said the more informed second organiser, who was painting a *Braveheart* face on a young piper.

"Who?"

"Boudicca."

"Boudicca?"

"Aye, the woman this woman is supposed to be." Organiser Two turned to me. "That's you, isn't it? You're the one who is going to sit on that horse?"

I was about to answer with a cryptic comment about facial hair and women when Organiser One stood up with a dramatic dump of her brush.

"No one will know who she is with a beard," said Organiser One. "They'll be wondering if it's a *he*, *she*, or even *it*."

"What is the point of that?" said Organiser Two.

"Point?" said Organiser One. "Mystery, keep 'em guessing."

"But I want to be recognised," I said, "reveal Lochgilphead's new goddess of belly dancing, not play Who's the Moron behind the Beard."

They looked at me like I was speaking German.

"What's dancing got to do with anything? You're here to scare, and a beard would really work," said Organiser One.

I was tempted to tell them to shove it when the young piper, with his face now in *Braveheart* paint, turned to me.

"You're riding the horse?"

I nodded.

"You've seen it?"

I shook my head but explained that according to many, it was so much better than expected.

He whistled through his teeth. "You're brave. My granny wouldn't even climb the ladder of a bunk bed let alone sit on that."

It was hard to tell behind the face paint whether the young piper was impressed or joking.

"I don't do bunk beds either," I said. "But I am sure it will be fine."

"Fine? That thing took months to make."

"Make?"

The *Braveheart* face looked at me. "Even the judo teacher refused to sit on it."

We stood outside the community center as *it* rolled up the car park. I heard the squeak of the hospital trolley before I saw it, and my heart began to pound. A giant papier mâché shire horse appeared from around the corner with its mouth, mid roar, open like a cave. It had a back as wide as a footpath and was supposedly rooted to the hospital trolley with three of its feet, the other being held in mid trot.

I looked about for an escape.

"That's yours," said Organiser One with an *I'll get you back for refusing to wear a beard* look. And before I had time to ditch my tartan and run, a table was wheeled across the tarmac for me to stand on.

"I don't do hospital trolleys," I muttered.

No one listened. Instead, I was ushered onto the table. I had an audience of orange-coat organisers watching, who, along the *Braveheart* face, egged me on . . .

You're doing great!

Sure you are!

You're so brave!

Do you think she needs a ladder?

Organiser Two placed a stool on the table. I stood on it as she held it and tried to ignore the shudder of the trolley.

I asked if it was safe, but no one answered . . .

Lochgilphead won't know what hit them when they see you!

You look amazing!

Made for the part!

Go easy, there's no brakes on that thing . . .

"What? No brakes?" I said with one leg poised across the vast back of the horse.

"Aye, but it's okay—we've got you, and we'll be with you all the way," said Organiser Two.

"And the pipe band is in front of you," said the *Braveheart* face with an earnest look. "They'll not let you roll down the hill."

I looked across at the band in the dark. Most of them were from the high school and were busy taking selfies. I had my doubts.

Organiser One handed me a fishing rod made into a spear, along with an "almost forgot this" comment. The spear wobbled in my hand.

"Be careful with the reins," she said, "they're just for show. In fact, I wouldn't hang on to them if I were you." She patted my foot. "Just pretend."

"What do I hang on to?" I said.

She laughed. "I know, it is cold, poor you, thank God for your tartan blanket." And then she left with her mobile glued to her ear, shouting at the rest of the procession to move it.

"Don't worry, we'll be back," said Organiser Two with a pat you'd give a dog. And before I had time to argue, she was away to sort out the judo team with the stool swinging in her hand. I watched as my only method of escape disappeared into the dark.

The Seated Yogi

I was sitting on the back of a horse so wide that it required a yoga position to balance. I couldn't move; I was trapped. I felt as vulnerable as a fly stuck in a web. I waited in the dark, alone and forgotten. Even the pipe band had disappeared. Apparently, a dog had run off with the pipe major's larger-than-life, talked-about-by-many sporran, and someone, somewhere, was trying to sort things out.

I felt like a child frozen on the back of an elephant waiting for her parents to return. I was immobilised on a horse as high as a fireman's ladder, trying to control a fishing rod that waved to whatever breeze blew. What was I thinking? The view was lousy, my face was now unrecognisable with blue paint, and my pelvis was locked into some sort of childbirth position that made even coughing uncomfortable.

"Having fun?" shouted Mavis from the rear.

I told Mavis I was an idiot, stupid to agree, and she laughed. "This," she said, gesturing with a coffee cup, "is yours at the finish line: extra whisky, extra cream, and extra strong."

"Cheers," I muttered.

She told me to enjoy, that everyone was waiting to see me, and that they all thought I was a good sport.

"Shout your lungs off," she said.

I asked her if she'd seen Rodger, and she said nothing. I asked her where in the crowd he was, and she still said nothing. Instead, she gave me yet another pat on my foot followed by a thumbs-up.

"I don't want to miss the primary school boat," she said. "The barbershop quartet are on it. They are singing Viking songs—dressed as Vikings."

Mavis had a thing for the baritone.

I watched her back disappear into the dark and waited.

Finally, I heard the roll of the drums in the distance as the pipe band warmed up. Two boys with faces still young enough to get excited about a McDonald's appeared.

"You're next," shouted one.

While the other reassured me that they wouldn't let go.

They grabbed the ropes and pulled as the pipe band began to blast a rousing "Flower of Scotland."

We were heading for the top of the main street with a braw view of the loch. I clung on with my flexible pelvis working overtime and my thighs gripping like a wrestler's. I could hear the crowd clapping and cheering as I searched for Rodger in the crowds.

Who's that fanny on the horse?

No idea.

One of the judo team?

Rugby player?

The boys pulled the horse to the top of the hill as the parade was called to a halt. The wind picked up speed, sending my spear into a frenzy. "What's the hold-up?" I shouted.

"The storyteller is taking longer than planned," said the boy. "Once she's finished, we can head off, and then the Celtic warriors will begin."

The judo team stood behind me. The connection between Celtic warriors and judo is a slim one, but apparently, with enough blue paint, it is believable. And the crowd loved them. They began to chant. The judo team, inspired by the chanting and the lack of adults, began to push, egging each other on. They were fed up waiting; they had had enough of a storyteller they couldn't hear.

Freedom! shouted a young voice from the crowd.

Bring on the warriors! shouted another.

"She's finished, let's go," shouted the lead.

"No she hasn't," shouted one of my rope holders. "There are still five verses to go."

Can't hear anything.

Me neither.

Is that clapping?

Definitely finished.

"Let's go," shouted the lead at the top of his voice.

Inspired by their leader, the judo team filled their lungs and let forth a war cry. The crowd joined in as the youth of Lochgilphead rampaged down the street like a kung fu film, past me and my brake-less trolley.

The rope holders didn't stand a chance.

"Stop," shouted one of the rope holders as the crowd swept past him. He grimly hung onto the rope until a girl raced past. She, lost in the moment and yelling, "You can take our homes, you can take our mobiles, but you will never take our freedom," grabbed him, and he lost his grip.

I watched him disappear into the distance.

With only one rope holder left, the trolley staggered, tilted, and began to roll, faster and faster . . .

"We've lost it," shouted the other boy, who vainly tried to hang on until he skidded on a chip wrapper and fell to the ground. I looked back to see him sprawled on the tarmac, arms outstretched, shouting, "Nooooo . . ."

The trolley picked up speed.

The players scattered like sheep as my trolley rampaged through the pipe band. I clung to the paper reins like my life depended on it, which was as much use as hanging on to toilet paper. One tug and the reins cascaded down the road, joining the rope holder sprawled across the tarmac.

I rolled down the street, my arms flapping about like the wings of a cartoon chicken. I looked as much like a great warrior as Marge Simpson and was now screaming like her.

I passed the pipe major. He, a round man of sixty, made a dive for the horse's leg, missed, and fell to the ground. Within an instant, he was up, running like a stuntman half his age. He hurled himself at the trolley, wrapped one arm around its leg, and then used his own legs as a break. His kilt flapped in the wind like a weather flag, revealing a true Scotsman with a fine set of jewels as impressive as his much-talked-about sporran . . .

I sailed, bumped, and skidded past the Viking boat, knocking over the quartet, a few bins, and a papier mâché beaver. The pipe major hung on, digging his heels into the ground.

"Come on, lads!" he shouted. "She's heading for the chip van! This thing will blow with all that fat."

The pipe major's words moved many men, who grabbed the trolley from all sides. They slowed the trolley down until, with a mere plop and a mountain of grunts, I landed on the green, just shy of the burger stand.

Not a roll was disturbed.

"Cheers," shouted Jimmie from the chip van.

The crowd cheered as they circled around the pipe major.

Well done, you!

Saved the day!

"Best parade ever," muttered an elderly woman, her eyes on the pipe major.

The reporter pushed his way through the crowd, thrust a microphone in the pipe major's face, and said, "What raced through your mind to take such a risk?"

The pipe major laughed. "My grandchildren—they come here every year. Didn't want to spoil it for them."

"You risked your life for your grandchildren?"

"And the chip van," said the pipe major. "You can't beat a good chip butty."

I walked back to the community center and collected my things. No one noticed as I walked by—without the horse, I was nothing and nobody.

I put my tartan blanket in my bag and stared at my blue face in the mirror.

Mavis, with a talent for appearing from nowhere, plonked a mug in front of me. "Something stronger?" she said.

I looked at her. "No one even knew it was me," I said.

"Probably just as well."

"Even the reporter."

"His son plays for the pipe band, I wouldn't take it personally."

I sighed and praised the gods, the universe, even karma.

"And Rodger?" I said. "Did he see me?"

"Rodger," said Mavis, "was held up, indisposed . . ."

"Oh?" I said.

"Yes. He was in the Argyll with the pipe major."

"Before or after?" I said.

"Oh, before. They were sharing a brandy," said Mavis. "The pipe major always has one before a parade."

Mavis followed with a vivid description of Bingo howling to the sound of the pipes warming up nearby.

"It was the smell of brandy that did it," she said. "Drove Bingo into a frenzy on a par with . . . that night."

I stared into the distance.

"Bingo made a beeline for the pipe major's sporran, and within minutes it was swiped, chewed, and dragged upstairs."

"I see."

"And Rodger followed . . ."

A toupee was sourced, brushed, and tossed in the pipe major's direction. And the pipe major, being an adaptable sort of bloke, made the best of things. He shouted to Rodger not to bother—but Rodger didn't hear.

Rodger surfaced hours later, clutching what looked like a mop head in one hand and a subdued Bingo in the other.

I wanted to kiss Bingo, or at least toss him a dog biscuit.

"Attention," I said, "is not always a great thing. I'm glad the major got it all."

Mavis looked surprised.

"I mean who would want to be remembered for almost destroying the chip van?"

THE RED CROSS SHOP AND THE CODPIECE

The codpiece, like a padded bra, often promises more than what is beneath.

George's codpiece is a magnificent piece of expanding equipment which, with the aid of a long-life battery, pulsated to music.

The straps are studded with green and red baubles. The tip (or "main event," as George likes to call it) sprung forth like a jack-in-the-box, presenting a bloodred, jewelled disco ball at the end with an almost *ta-da*–like quality, spurring a woman to forget her "darling, I've a headache" as soon as she saw it.

George had first spied it in the Red Cross charity shop.

He walked past on his way to the butcher's and there it was in the window passing itself off as abstract art. He stopped and stared at the red tip just shy of the mannequin's askew wig and soon forgot about his pork chops.

The charity shop was run by Elsa and Karin, two women who had spent their lives making scones for the Women's Rural Instute, (WRI). The only codpieces they had seen, apart from ballet on Television, were Henry VII's armor during a school trip to London (which wasn't yesterday) and the amateur dramatics society's one and only attempt at Shakespeare—as Hamlet as camp as Liberace who wore his codpiece like a hairpiece and, according to the local paper's witticism, had "as much acting ability as a glass of water."

The codpiece was hanging on the doorknob in a Marks and Spencer bag when Elsa and Karin arrived.

Elsa, with a quick glance, thought it was a joke coat hanger, which started her off on a rant that Karin had heard many times. In fact, the mere mention of "hangers" often led to her plugging in her headphones and nodding like a Chinese cat doll.

"What's this," said Elsa, "another of those friggin' crochet-covered coat hangers?"

Karin, shop keys poised, huffed a silent "here we go."

"I mean who came up with that idea?" said Elsa. "They are about as much use as one of those crochet toilet roll covers."

Karin opened the door.

"Surely there are better ways to use up spare wool than crocheting pointless covers," said Elsa.

Karin marched into the dark shop and switched on the lights. She sighed. "Must we go down that coat hanger road again?"

Elsa thumped the bag on the counter. "A toilet roll is a toilet roll, a coat hanger's a coat hanger—they're not genitals that need covering up," she said.

"Must we move on to genitals as well?" muttered Karin.

Elsa watched as Karin switched on the till and opened up the back door.

"They should be banned," she said to herself.

Karin flicked the Closed sign to Open and then stopped. "If you really feel that strongly about it, why don't you write to the WRI —or better still leave, join the Women's Guild?"

"Guild?" Elsa jolted. "Have you seen their bottle stall? Not a wine in sight. They have no idea what the public want."

Karin fingered her mp3 player, wondering what she had *downloaded recently*.

"One as bad as the other," muttered Elsa. "As for *her* who runs the Guild . . . I see enough of her in here."

Karin lifted the bag from under Elsa's clutches and peered in.

Elsa flicked on the kettle. "She's living in the Dark Ages"—she checked the fridge for milk—"saving the world with homemade jam."

"I don't think Her from the Guild believes in jam saving things," said Karin.

"Her last bottle stall was full of 'em," said Elsa. "As if anyone is going to spend a tenner on raffle tickets for a jar of strawberry jam."

Karin muttered about "homemade" as Elsa ranted on about the bottle stall.

"She's been warned," said Elsa, "if her next bottle stall doesn't make any money, she's out . . . for good. I mean who gets sacked from the Guild?"

Karin, feigning listening, pulled the codpiece into the light. She gasped.

"I don't think it's a coat hanger."

"What?" said Elsa.

"I said I don't think it's a coat hanger."

Elsa looked up from the fridge and stared at the apparition suspended from Karin's hand as the morning sun twinkled on its baubles. She whistled through her teeth. "Talk about genitals—that's big enough for an elephant's."

Karin read the note attached to the belt. "It's from that belly dancing teacher."

"Well, that explains it," muttered Elsa. "Anyone who talks about pelvic tilts and TENA pads in the same sentence as a latte is bound to be a bit, well . . . free with things."

"Hmm . . . she's written, 'Have fun,'" muttered Karin.

"Told you, as free as a nudist colony," said Elsa.

"'Open your mind and give your pelvis a good seeing to,'" Karin read aloud.

"Completely pelvic obsessed," said Elsa.

"'Fulfill your fantasy,'" read Karin.

Elsa flicked the tip of the codpiece; it sprung into action. "It's not one of those vibrators, is it?"

"'Build a bonfire, dance al fresco, and discover that goddess within,'" Karin read.

"She's been on the home brew," muttered Elsa. She looked at her pal. "Why don't you put it on?"

"What?" said Karin.

"It's Monday," muttered Elsa. "No one comes in on a Monday, even *Her* from the Guild."

Her from the Guild was the new Red Cross store manager. She had only been in the role for three months and had managed to lose every volunteer apart from Elsa and Karin. She'd been given the job without any experience beyond a few hours in her daughter's coffee shop. Some say the daughter pulled a few strings, couldn't bear another hour of her mother's lukewarm lattes served with a temperance sermon that turned even the most loyal of customers away.

"Why don't you?" said Karin, handing the codpiece to Elsa.

Elsa shoved it back.

"Me? My size? Where am I to put it, around my neck? No, definitely you."

Karin jangled the codpiece. "It looks contractable."

They stared at the so-called "one-size-fits-all" pelvic apparition swaying before them.

"Not that contractable," muttered Elsa.

Karin said nothing.

"And you're the one with superb hips," said Elsa.

Karin muttered a "hmmm."

"Even that belly dancing teacher said you were a natural," said Elsa; she could see she was winning her pal around.

Karin threw her a half-hearted *pfff* look.

"She said you could make hessian flow with your hip moves," said Elsa.

Karin looked at her pal.

"She wanted to know why you didn't come back to her class. Had plans for you." Elsa caught Karin's eye. "Imagine that thing—with those shimmies you love to do."

"Oh all right then," snapped Karin.

Elsa flicked on the kettle as Karin slid into the changing room.

Elsa's phone pinged a text.

"It's *her* from the Guild," shouted Elsa. "She's wanting something for the next bottle stall!"

"Should I take off my jumper?" said Karin.

"No, seriously, she does," said Elsa. She scrolled down the Queen's

Speech of a message, skimming quickly through the "how to improve things" sermon.

Her from the Guild managed from a distance, occasionally calling in to rubbish Karin's latest color-coordinated clothes rack or Elsa's innovative window display; she even Skyped once, until Elsa switched her off mid rant.

"What about my shoes?" shouted Karin. "Should I take 'em off too?"

Elsa stopped. "Jesus."

"What was that?" yelled Karin. "Shoes too much?"

"She's coming here this afternoon," shouted Elsa.

"Who?" said Karin.

"Guess," yelled Elsa.

"I thought she was on holiday, taking in the ballet somewhere hot," said Karin.

Elsa sighed. "Not anymore."

"Jesus," muttered Karin.

"Apparently, there's an issue with our 'so-called window display.' Something to do with our out-of-date . . ." Elsa stopped.

"Out-of-date what?" said Karin.

"Err . . . mannequin," muttered Elsa.

"There nothing out of date about *my* mannequin," snapped Karin. "I used it for years before I brought it here."

Elsa waited; she knew there was more.

"It's retro, evocative, quiche."

"Don't you mean niche?" said Elsa.

"That window would be nothing without my mannequin," said Karin, "and if that's the thanks I get—"

"I know, she can shove it," muttered Elsa to herself.

"—we should give her something to choke on," said Karin.

"Exactly," said Elsa.

"Something as outrageous as her stupid demands."

"I know," shouted Elsa.

"Something to . . . you know . . . stop her in tracks—shut her up."

"Something to put her right in her place," said Elsa.

"How about this?" Karin swished the curtains open.

Elsa stared at Karin's pelvis decorated like a joker's hat as the kettle, bubbling unattended, filled the shop with steam.

"Jesus!" she muttered.

Karin wiggled.

The codpiece jumped to life, making Elsa *feel a bit funny.*

Childhood memories flashed back to a ballet concert in Glasgow where Elsa, sitting painfully on a hard seat, wondered (between bouts of boredom) what all *that* Rudolf Nureyev fuss was about. To a sporty ten-year-old, men in tights were as stupid as her mother's hairstyle, and a bulge between the legs was as intriguing as a pickled egg recipe.

Karin twirled a few times, the codpiece swaying like a jewelled palm tree, expanding and contracting.

Perhaps I should revisit Rudolf Nureyev? thought Elsa.

Karin finished with a robust pelvic thrust.

Or even some younger dancer? thought Elsa.

Neither saw Harry, an elderly gentleman, pass by.

He, in the middle of pondering the butcher's latest leek-and-mushroom sausages, stopped as he caught the pulsating burble shoot past his side vision.

Harry turned to catch Karin mid pelvis thrust.

He stared.

Karin waved.

Harry, like a stunned Labrador, was mesmerised, sausages as far from his thoughts as last night's toenail trimmings.

Karin, who according to many was still a catch, had the sort of pelvic thrust that could set a man's heart thumping. Especially a man whose only contact with a woman was having his blood pressure checked.

Karin wiggled with a giggle.

"I saw one in the war," he shouted.

"Aye right," she shouted.

"I did," he shouted back. "There's a lot to Hitler folk don't know about."

Elsa's phone lit up, and a Dolly Parton ringtone echoed through the shop; the codpiece bounced into action.

Harry chuckled, setting off a round of coughing, as Karin twirled with her best *I'm looking for a shag* look.

Elsa's phoned stopped, the codpiece flopped, and Karin, mid pose, tried not to look silly.

Elsa fumbled to find more music.

"Hurry up," muttered Karin as Harry tapped on the window and pulled out his phone.

"Do it again, they'll never believe me at the butcher's."

Elsa found a Status Quo song and, mid cursing her husband's lousy taste in music, flicked it on.

Down, down, deeper and down . . .

The codpiece went mental.

A couple of hours and several Status Quo albums later, the codpiece was swinging from the window like a pornographic wind chime just shy of a seventies mannequin dressed like something out a sex shop, and Her from the Guild was livid.

Elsa and Karin had spent all morning redoing the window with Harry videoing (or "helping," as he called it).

They figured if Her from the Guild was coming for her usual get-rid-of-the-volunteers lecture, then they may as well get their money's worth . . .

They were going out in style.

The girls threw everything they could at the window: leather belts disguised as whips, boots, bras, underpants, aprons—they went to town, relying on Harry's knowledge of all things pornographic, as the only dubious things they had seen were Barbara Windsor's breast in a *Carry On* film and the odd nude in the local art show.

Karin and Elsa learnt many things: mainly that when it came to sex, Harry's memory was as clear as Highland Spring water, while theirs was as muddy as a cappuccino.

Finally finished and satisfied and Status Quo switched to a *Seventies Greatest Hits* album, the three stopped to admire their handywork with a coffee.

"It's a work of art," muttered Harry, tucking into a scone just as Her from the Guild flounced through the door.

By the time George passed by the shop, Her from the Guild had been inside long enough to not only throw a wobbly but also destroy much of the window ambience by covering the mannequin with a crochet blanket, causing a coughing fit from Harry.

As Harry recovered with a glass of water, George stared at the codpiece. The crochet blanket slung over the mannequin gave it a more avant-garde look, and his Beatrice could be very avant-garde.

He had known Beatrice since the black-and-white TV days, and she was a woman easily pissed off. This piece just might tip her over the edge from platonic to . . . well . . .

He stared at the bloodred knob.

It'll make her weak at the knees, he thought. *It's making me weak just now.*

He spotted the elderly gentleman by the shop counter recovering. Then he heard Her from the Guild, a woman as pious as the Pope and as sober as the temperance movement. In fact, if there were a local temperance group, she'd be running it; she was so against alcohol she had even refused George's offer of a malt whisky for her latest bottle stall.

And that would have made a bucket of money, but then again, thought George, *maybe it was because she recognised me . . . from another time.*

George eyed the codpiece. It had as much chance of surviving under her clutches as her bottle stall did of making money.

He had to do something.

He knew the Guild had nearly sacked her, given her one last chance to run the bottle stall . . . and he also knew of a time, years ago, when Her from the Guild was anything but pious.

He smiled to himself. That codpiece was all but his. With a friendly tap on the door and his best casual saunter, George entered.

No one noticed.

Her from the Guild was in full throttle, claiming that the so-called art in the window had as much to do with art as a bottle stall had with alcohol.

"There's a bonfire with that thing's name on it," she yelled.

The others tried to argue, but she, dismissing all arguments of it being "one of a kind," ploughed through her speech like a minister preaching fire and brimstone to the masses.

"This is a charity shop, not an Ann Summers shop," she yelled.

"Ann Summers?" mouthed Elsa to Karin and Harry. "How would she know?"

"I know about Ann Summers," said Her from the Guild. "I know about all these things. I was once like you—a heathen, a lost soul . . ."

"Hello, Carisa," said George.

She stopped. *No one had called her that for years.*

The two girls looked at each other with a *that's her name?* look.

"I see you moved on from coat hangers and tea sets." He paused. "Carisa."

"Well, not exactly," she muttered.

They looked at each other like they had a past . . . a past that hadn't ended well.

"The last time I saw you, you were trying to sell raffle tickets for the bottle stall with jars of jam and a bottle of Sarson's vinegar."

"Don't call me Carisa," sniffed Her from the Guild.

"You made enough to what," said George, "pay for the rent of stall?" He paused for effect. "Carisa."

"I said don't call me that," said Her from the Guild.

They looked at each other. George knew that he could say more, he could tell all; he waited.

Her from the Guild fumbled with the till and muttered something about the shop being closed.

George didn't move. "I hear you're doing another bottle stall, for the Gala Day," he said.

The room was silent, the girls and Harry poised.

What's next? mouthed Karin.

"And?" she said, attempting to hold her own.

"We've been here before, haven't we?" said George. "Another time, another place?"

She blushed.

"Jesus," Elsa mouthed to Karin.

Harry chuckled, setting off a round of coughing.

George patted his back, making the coughing worse.

Harry waved him to stop.

"I've a few tricks up my sleeve this time," said Her from the Guild.

"Tricks? It's a bottle stall. Throw in a few bottles of wine and malt whisky and you're laughing," said Karin.

"Yes, well . . . there's more to it than that," said Her from the Guild.

"But is there?" said George.

"Well, I . . ." She caught George's eye and stopped.

A few days later, as George surprised, seduced, and entertained Beatrice into bed with his codpiece, Elsa and Karin were celebrating in the Argyll Hotel.

They had left the charity shop.

Harry had assured them that he had seen plenty, knew what he was talking about, and was happy to help in an advisory capacity.

George had been generous.

"You're welcome to the codpiece any time for a template," he said. "Anything to spread the joy of a codpiece."

Elsa and Karin had a plan that not only would make great use of Karin's retro mannequin but would lead the two of them into a world far more entertaining than selling under that *pain in the arse* from the Guild.

They were going to make and sell codpieces on the internet, starting with designs inspired by George's codpiece.

George offered to make a donation to the bottle stall in exchange for the codpiece. It was large enough to impress those in the Guild, and Her from the Guild had no choice but to accept.

She had a past, a past that she wanted kept there. A time when she drank too much; she got so drunk at a Gala Day she drank the whisky from the bottle stall and danced on the table, hurling the pickled egg jars into the crowd.

Some would call it a turning point.

It was a lifetime ago, and George had promised never to tell, but as she handed in his donation to the Guild, Her from the Guild realised that perhaps bottle stalls were best left to someone comfortable with a bottle of whisky inches from their hand.

A few months later, at the Gala Day, Her from the Guild stood behind the burger stand, frying onions. At first, she didn't see Karin and Elsa set up their stand—until the mannequin was erected. Mid peeling an onion, Her from the Guild stopped as a crochet codpiece was wrapped around the mannequin's pelvis. Elsa and Karin had gone for a more subtle, comic element for the family day out.

Not subtle enough, thought Her from the Guild, until she spied George with Beatrice heading for her stall.

He caught her eye.

But then again, crochet is not so bad, she told herself. *It has a certain restrained charm about it.* And she pulled out another onion to peel.

AND NOW FOR SOME SCI-FI

INTRODUCTION

The is nothing greater than man's imagination,it just needs a little tweaking now and then.

The idea came from kilts, bagpipes, and an overheard conversation that only a man would have. The sort of conversation that involved various bits of the body that only a man would know about.

"If your eyes could be anywhere in your body apart from the eye socket, where would that be?"

I was aroused, excited, and amused as I listened to where and why.

I guess having a swinging appendage between your legs changes how you see things, a thought which sparked me to write from a man's point of view and turn stereotyping on its head.

I was trying to write "Thirty Seconds" at the time, a story about a sexually frustrated man trying to seduce his lesbian wife by writing an erotic sci-fi novel *and* a pantomime. The sci-fi grew arms, legs, and other bits of anatomy, and my erotica writing, which was as erotic as a cold fish, metamorphosed into a half-baked satire. I finally changed the male sci-fi characters to elderly women, and voila, I had found *my* story.

Impressing Bunnie is a follow-on from the first book, *Rebel without a Clue.* Mex, "our heroine," is stuck on Earth and gives her account of catching a ferry with her new earthling subjects.

The Foot Rub started as outtakes from *Rebel without a Clue,* when I had no idea who should tell the story and was experimenting with different character's viewpoints.

The other stories—*An Android's Christmas, The Lady in the Box,* and *The Polishing of a Knob*—are follow-ons from *Rebel without a Bra* and *Rebel without a Crew,* the second and third books in the series. The stories are written in the voice of Pete, a robot inspired by Stephen Fry in *Jeeves and Wooster*.

IMPRESSING BUNNIE

Hindsight is as elusive as a decent bra and can be as uncomfortable as a bad one.

I stared at the ferry sailing into the distance; we had missed it by minutes. The others, in fear of "fading away" during a twenty-minute journey on the Clyde, made for the Aloha Coffee Shack while I made a start on my log. Pete was sitting beside me, legs crossed and looking scarily comfortable—like a secretary.

He scribbled the date on the top of his pad and looked up. "When you're ready, ma'am."

"This is not going to be pleasant, Pete," I said.

"Ma'am."

"I am not going to mince words," I said.

"Feel free to mince, ma'am."

"I am not sure who I am writing to or how I can even send it."

"Mere details," said Pete. "Best to get *it* off your chest while in the comfort of a limo."

"It?" I said.

"Definitely," said Pete.

I stared at the couple in the car in front; would they have an *it* on their chests?

"My pen is poised, ma'am," said Pete.

I began with a few introductory updates about the ol' fella and

Johnny while Pete flicked through a bundle of pens like it was a selection of earrings. I flashed him one of my *I thought you said you were ready* looks and began . . .

"I have worked my boots off for our planet, and for what?"

"Best not to start with a question," said Pete, "it only confuses those in the know."

"To amble through this testosterone-pumped planet in search of a boring man who does nothing but laminates about the intricacies of a woman?"

"I think you will find that it's *laments*, ma'am," said Pete.

"A man who is short yet tall, possibly an alcoholic, who may be at the end of some pickled egg of a journey across the wilds of Scotland . . ."

"Ma'am, it is a mere twenty-minute journey, and there will be coffee and snacks."

". . . and thanks to those in charge—who 'know best'—I have been sent with a piece of equipment as useless as dentures on a puppet . . ."

"If ma'am could dictate just a tad slower," said Pete, "I may be able to get the finer details of your said . . . lament."

". . . a piece of equipment that grows legs, buggers off, and explodes, leaving me dictating to a robot completely up himself."

"Android, ma'am," muttered Pete.

"I feel betrayed, led up the patio, and tossed over the side like a used teabag. Beryl and her promises . . . I should have known better. Beryl is the plug you stand on: useful, necessary, but, when the wrong way up, as painful as Pete and his ramblings about chest relieving."

Pete sighed. "Perhaps ma'am is still hung over from the ol' fella's tablet?"

"I feel fine," I said. "A little shaky, but alert and clear minded."

"A sugar rush is no easy thing," said Pete, "and coming down can be as treacherous as one of Bunnie's *let me top up your drink*s."

Ignoring Pete, I continued . . .

The first time I saw Beryl was years ago, back in the days when egg popping was at the experimental stage. I was staring at the fish aquarium on the wall, wondering if fish felt pain, when Beryl's voice boomed from nowhere.

"We'll call her Mex," she said. "It's short and to the point—just like her nose."

No one said anything; the room was so silent you could hear a fish gulp, even though she was trying to be funny.

"She's the first of a few," said Beryl.

"So you keep saying," muttered one of the many scientists, or *white coats*, as they were known.

"And she needs a name that is something special."

"A name like a blender," said the white coat, causing a few to chuckle.

"*Mex* is new, crisp, and easy to spell," said Beryl.

"And blends at five different speeds."

"Yes, well, when she goes down in the great records of history," said Beryl, "no one will be spelling her name wrong."

"It's a baby," said another white coat. "Her future is as blank as a man's appendage."

The scientists fell about laughing.

"Very funny. It must be absolutely fabulous to have both brains and wit," said Beryl.

"We do our best; why not crack a joke along with a code?"

Beryl let out one of her infamous *who's in charge?* coughs and continued. "As you well know, Mex is from the new batch of eggs. And it's in her genes to be great—there are no comedians in her lineage."

A few muttered as Beryl's pale face loomed into view like a vertical sunrise. Her blond hair was piled up high, like scoops of ice cream in a cone, with a tiny pink bow stuck in the middle. I watched her face block out my view of the fish and wondered if the bow would fall off if I tapped it. I stretched to touch.

Beryl tugged at my finger. "You're the first"—she smiled—"but you're not the last."

I grabbed her finger and clung to the warm flesh until she pulled free and moved on to the next baby capsules—babies from the same batch of eggs.

"You're special," she muttered to one of them.

"Ow, that was my finger—you can go back," she said to another.

"Really, ma'am, give her a try. It's not even been a week."

"She needs more work," said Beryl.

"But work at this stage . . . is it high on the agenda?"

The room fell silent as the scientist was ushered outside.

Five of us were incubated that summer, and we were, according to *Her Leadership*, so special that we remained in the incubation center and were not, like every other generation, farmed out to a grandmother. Instead, we were to watch, absorb, and ask. We grew up under the eyes of women in white coats clutching test tubes and looking under microscopes. And when we were old enough, we sat on the workbenches watching, questioning, and sometimes recording as they investigated along with cracking the odd joke.

"See this?" said one white coat, stabbing at a Petri dish containing moldy Brie. "In a few days' time, opening this will clear the room."

"Wonderful."

"Well, I could empty a building for days with this piece. Just one wave—one particle."

"Marvelous."

"Methinks you jest."

"Jest, me? In a white coat—how could that be possible?"

It was amusing until I was about fourteen . . .

Beryl liked to burst into the laboratory like there was a crisis somewhere. She spent her time pulling at logbooks and telling the ladies in white to answer our every question, "as my girls are our future."

Beryl loved looking over our records and telling us we were *all special* and had a place *in the scheme of things*—except for me. Apparently, I had as much insight as a pizza. While the other four tugged at her jacket with questions on energy replacement and egg popping and bribed her with polished apples and smiley faces, I remained aloof. I wanted to kick things into oblivion, especially her bow. Over the years, I had watched that pink bow grow so large it took over the front of her beehive like a giant butterfly, and I dreamed of a kick so high I could remove it in one move. Nobody in the lab had a clue about my thoughts.

Back then, in Beryl's pink-bow days, she was a Voted In apprentice and desperate to move up. She often talked of the *leader's chair* and the *room with a view* and how one day she would be there with her picture on the "wall of leaders."

"A picture is just a picture: easily removed," said one of the prodigies.

"Not mine," said Beryl. "I'll be running things and making all the right decisions."

"Right decisions are only right upon reflection," said another prodigy.

Beryl threw her a look. "One day I will be in charge, basking in my glorious leadership skills and looking at the view from the top."

"And what's wrong with the view here?" said one of the white coats.

We looked outside at the slag heap by the bike shed, and for the first time, no one could think of a joke.

Of course, when Legless rebelled, it all changed.

I was standing in Beryl's office, at the time a full-fledged teenager, explaining why learning the ropes of energy replacement didn't really "gel" for me. Beryl, a woman who had no idea about the art of *gelling*, was anything but impressed.

"I don't care if energy replacement *gels* or not; the whole point of your existence is to benefit the planet, to speed up the process of science. You have been programmed to get excited about equations, chemistry, and sparks plugs, not to fail every exam like a dyslexic half-wit male."

She tossed my last exam across the desk. "You are supposed to be a prodigy."

I stared at the pink bow in her hair, now the size of a dinner plate. *Just one kick . . .*

"What has happened to you?" she asked.

Nothing. I have always been like this.

"Explain yourself."

I looked at the woman who *claimed* to be on my side. "Your prodigies spell like spell checkers and multiply in minutes while I'm still trying to decipher letters from numbers."

"And?"

"I just don't think like that."

"It is time you started."

"I prefer to kick and things," I muttered.

"So I heard."

"Ma'am," I said, "I kicked a mere test tube . . . destined for the recycler."

Beryl threw me one of her looks, sighed, and then, as she always did at such moments, made for the window and stared in silence. "There are only so many times one can stretch the 'Science and Stuff' budget for fumigating," she finally muttered.

"They were laughing at me," I said. "Shouldn't I stand up for myself?"

"All scientists laugh."

"That is exactly my point. I don't. I am not like them; nothing is funny to me." *I paused for effect.* "You understand?"

Beryl turned to me. "Yes, well, kicking and things were the downfall of men—have you learnt nothing?"

"But fresh air and punching help . . . you should try it."

"Enough. You are to go back, work on your sums, and build the next great spark plug. I will hear no more."

Beryl's face was flushed, and her bow was bobbing excessively as she stomped about the office. I knew that I had pushed her to the limit, that I was on my last leg—although she had been telling me that for ages.

I stared at Beryl's aquarium. It was huge, taking up most of the wall, with overfed fish loitering about the bottom and belching.

"Trying to fit in is not easy when you are the butt of jokes," I said, "especially when you don't ever realise it's a joke."

Beryl had no intention of listening. Instead, she continued on with her never-ending "if you don't get it together" sermon, and I was just waiting for the "this is your last chance" bit when an insistent knock interrupted Beryl mid flow.

"Ma'am, we have an incident . . ."

I watched Beryl march out of the room, *thank beetroot.* Soon she was shouting.

"Who the pickled egg does he think he is?"

"It is a rebellion, ma'am—of sorts. Best to take things calmly."

"Rebellion, for what? I don't understand—they are fed and watered. What more do they want?"

Beryl left the building soon after that, my exam results forgotten and tossed in the bin and me spared another lecture.

Later that day, Beryl took to her *penthouse pad*. She threw every pink belt, shoe, jacket, and hair bow over the side of her minimalist patio and, as they cascaded to the ground, she shouted, "Vengeance is very fine or Legless is a bottle of wine." No one was sure which, as they were too busy dodging the fallout—apparently a shoe from twenty stories plus lands like a missile—but when she appeared with her hair dyed black, everyone knew she meant business and Legless was done for.

A few days later, Beryl, sporting her new *black* look, appeared at my bunk bed.

"I think," she said, "your talents are better suited to boots and training."

The other girls looked up, rubbing their eyes, and gasped. *Beryl, first thing in the morning, in the bunk room?*

"Ma'am?" muttered one.

Beryl held up a hand to silence her.

For the first time ever, I felt important.

"I knew you were something special," said Beryl. "But I never thought it would be kicking and the like."

"Kicking?" muttered another of the girls.

"Yes." Beryl turned to her other so-called prodigies. "Some use microscopes to change the world; others, like Mex here, use"—she patted my six-pack—"brawn."

"Anyone can do sit-ups."

"Yes, but how many can, with the precision of one kick, remove a Petri dish lid from its dish without one crack?"

"That's stupid."

"Not anymore," said Beryl. She looked at me. "Pack your things and come with me."

"Ma'am," said Pete. "I think Bunnie has arrived."

I had already spied her in the side mirror—waltzing across the car park clutching a couple of Aloha Coffee bags—and I had decided to continue with my dictation. Bunnie's the sort of woman who is curious, un-shock-able, and good at keeping things to herself—so she tells me—and I kind of liked the idea of her hearing about my heroic deeds.

She tapped at the window; I unwound it and she poked her head inside.

"Roll and sausage, anyone?"

Pete jumped at the chance.

"Your story is very interesting," Bunnie said, passing a roll to Pete.

I wondered how much she had heard and if I needed to repeat myself.

"I thought there was something funny about you, but I never thought it was because you came from a different planet—where a womb is a Petri dish."

I looked at Bunnie. "It is more complicated than that."

"You would never know—you look just like me."

"I wouldn't say that," I muttered.

"So human."

"Well, yes," I said, "but in a much more refined sort of way."

Bunnie slid into the front with a "no need to be rude" huff as I told Pete that we might as well continue . . . because, as Pete put it, "the cat had escaped the bag."

Bunnie chuckled into her sausage as Pete, still engrossed in the white package, began to unwrap with way too many *oohs* and *aahs* for a robot. I mean a square sausage is hardly a sight to behold.

"The others will be back soon," I said, "and there is more on my chest, so to speak—so if you are ready?"

"Take your time," said Bunnie. "They decided on Chinese, you have all day to *refine* your log."

"Chinese?"

"Bit like Indian, ma'am, but sweeter," said Pete.

"Indian?"

"Yes, Sheila from Bombay," said Bunnie, "sweeter and easier on the digestion."

"I see," I said. "I forgot that digestion on Earth still has its problems."

I caught a look from Bunnie in the rearview mirror and continued . . .

"It seemed that I was the first and the last *man spy*, and the 'kicking and punching' gene had started and ended with me—I had a lot to live up to. Of course, Beryl continued to try and control; her sermons never stopped. She told me not to get too full of myself. 'You have a position of great honor,' she said. 'An honor new and elusive, which no one must know of—your name must be but a mere whisper . . .'"

"Great roll," muttered Pete. "So juicy."

"Absolutely, Pete, nothing refined about a delicious hot sausage, each bite is squelchier than the last . . ."

"Soon," I said, "I became the woman with a whip no one looked at, who could silence a room with a couple of flicks and, of course, a look. But now, thanks to *they who must be right*, my whip has been folded away—*incognito* as a pair of underpants—as we search for a man who thinks the internet is bugged."

"Which it is," said Pete.

"Really? I thought he was paranoid," said Bunnie, wiping the corners of her mouth.

"How did you think we learnt about you on Earth," I said, "in a library?"

"Well, actually, I never thought about it, but a library sounds like a great place to start."

I explained to Bunnie how the men destroyed the libraries years ago when they were *going under*—losing control. "They bombed the libraries with flour bombs," I said, "and threw the books onto barbeques wearing plastic aprons with 'just for a laugh' slashed across their stomachs."

"The plastic aprons were never proven," said Pete.

"I thought the scientists had all the laughter genes," said Bunnie.

"The laughter gene has spread further than that," said Pete. "Some of us have found humor in your so-called sitcoms."

I told Pete not to start with the sitcoms as I caught Bunnie's eye yet again in the rearview mirror. "We're not big on emotion where I come from; in fact, watching a child cry is enough to turn my stomach, and as for laughter, that reminds me of the early years in the lab . . ."

Bunnie looked surprisingly unimpressed.

"Besides," I said, "I have the days of great *man spying* to dictate. I mean I haven't even started on how I saved the planet—filling the gym with enough men to energise for years."

I looked at Bunnie. My story had twists and turns all in my favor, and she wasn't even listening now; she was flicking through her phone, searching for the ferry times while muttering about me putting her "off her sausage."

"I saved the planet," I said. "I single-handedly captured every one of Legless's followers. I tracked them down like a terrier at a rat farm."

"There is no such thing, ma'am."

"Well, a terrier at a rabbit thing . . ."

"Everyone," said Bunnie, "and what about Legless? You never managed to track him."

"Legless was different," I said. "He and Beryl had an understanding."

Bunnie didn't hear; she was too busy swearing about the lack of internet and how thanks to last night's "printing incident"—an incident apparently more important than me saving the planet—she couldn't find the timetable so she could make "connections for things."

"If only you lot had behaved yourselves," snapped Bunnie.

The night before, Pete and DJ had tussled over the printer, which had led to an undignified bout of name-calling until Bunnie's dog jumped in. She had grabbed the off-peak timetables and demolished them with such relish that even I wouldn't go near her. She spent ten minutes growling like a bear while spitting out bits of paper, and soon the floor was covered in wet, limp specks of white.

Pete blamed DJ and Bunnie's whisky pouring, DJ blamed Pete and Bunnie's slippery floor, but neither had the balls to blame Izzie. Who, after she finished the timetables, had jumped on top of the printer, refusing to let anyone go near it; she'd even nipped my fingers.

I told Beryl that the incident had little to do with me, and that I wasn't one of anyone's *lot* but more a sort of "one-off heroic figure to be honored, feared, or at least talked about," but she wasn't interested until I mentioned Izzie.

"Oh, now you're blaming her," huffed Bunnie. "How fickle you all must be on your *refined* planet."

I stared at Bunnie. Her mood swings were as easy to understand as the Chinese takeaway menu she had tossed into the back of the limo. I told her so, and she stomped out of the car.

Pete told me that being a "told you so" sort of a person didn't go down well on Earth and was looking rather smug until I pointed out that he was doing the same thing . . .

Pete then accused me of "rattling Bunnie's cage," an unfamiliar expression which, thanks to Bunnie—now pacing outside on her phone—I got the gist of straightaway.

"How long is that friggin' Chinese gonna be?" she snapped. "At this rate we're gonna need to stay the night . . ." Pause. "Oh you have, have you . . ." Bunnie sighed. "Well, if he is like any of your other friends . . ." She rolled her eyes. "Well, free is not the be-all and end-all . . ." Then she let out a full-blown laugh, rattling the beads resting on her chest like jumping beans. "Of course, Donnie darling," she said. "As you say, boys will be . . ."

I watched Bunnie let out another, more hair-raising laugh, and I wondered what was so amusing about her Donnie and why she would rather talk on her phone than listen to my heroic deeds. I mean I had stories that could go on for hours, days. I'm sure, given half the chance, I could amuse, maybe even rattle Bunnie's beans . . . I mean how interesting can a man be? But would she give me the chance?

I never said anything; I was beginning to realise that on Earth, saying and thinking were two different things and were best kept that way until all information was gathered, sifted, and—dare I say it—discussed with a robot.

I looked across at my so-called Android; he was staring out of the windshield, sipping the remains of a latté with a wistful look. "Never trust a dog that can balance on a printer," he said, "it's not natural," which I thought was rich coming from a robot. He tossed the last of his roll to the seagulls, and we watched as they squawked over the remains.

"It is common here," he said, "to feed the birds."

"Really?" I said. "Doesn't this 'good-to-go' food give them indigestion?"

"Only a vindaloo," said Pete.

The pier flooded with open-mouthed gulls, screeching and nipping at each other while moving closer to Bunnie. We watched as one swooped past her head while two tugged over the last of sausage, completely ignoring her foot . . .

"Who the eff threw that?" shouted Bunnie and then went for a kick, skidding on the roll and cursing, "Bollocks and pickled eggs." Pete laughed as she grabbed the rail and caught her balance, and for the first time, I could see why. Then, when Bunnie shouted, "Thought you didn't find anything funny," I snorted—a new experience which I hoped to never repeat.

Bunnie then began to shout about "laughing on the other side of a face," and Pete was just on the verge of explaining when she shouted that the ferry was coming in and where the "so and so" was Don?

"We're coming," Don shouted from the rear of the car park.

And as I watched the others running in the side mirror, I realised my moment had come and gone without making a dent in Bunnie's armor. She hadn't asked me one question about my adventures—not the slightest interest—but when Don arrived on the scene, she was all over him with "where have you been" questions.

"You nearly missed it," I said as he jumped into the driver's seat.

Bunnie jumped in beside him. "Impossible," she said and caught my eye in the rearview mirror. "Only refined people from refined planets miss things. My Donnie has perfect timing, just like a terrier at a rat farm."

"What?" Don asked. "There is no such thing."

"A terrier on a printer," I said.

AN ANDROID'S CHRISTMAS

Pulling a cracker can sometimes lead to more than a paper hat.

December 2018—The Pedestrian and the Stuffed Turkey

Bunnie says Christmas is "all about cheese, alcohol, and spending time with the sort of friends that don't require *standing on ceremony*."

Woody says Christmas is "a time for TV repeats, stuffed turkey, and a new supply of socks."

Either way, it seems Christmas requires a lot of time spending money and waiting in car queues.

Mex and Bunnie threw themselves into the festive spirit with a quick scoot around a twenty-four-hour Asda.

"Let's give this saving-the-planet thing a rest for a day," said Bunnie, heading for all things meaty.

"Throw in some tablet and I am yours," said Mex from behind a trolley full of cheese.

Two hours and a full-to-bursting trolley later, Mex was out of her box on sugar. A complete sugar addict, she had munched her way through Asda's finest while checking out the children's section, trying out the fairy lights section, and wandering through the dispensary section fingering the odd tube with a *what the pickle is this?*

Asda to Mex was like a porn shop to a sixteen-year-old, and she had just about as much self-control. She ripped into the sweet stuff with a gay abandonment I had never seen before, all under the excuse of working out the difference between tablet, fudge, toffee, and chocolate. By the time they had hit the checkout, she was as high as a Planet Hy Man penthouse. And by the time Bunnie had left the car park and paused at the pedestrian crossing, Mex was laughing hysterically, until she saw what had stopped the traffic.

We have no sugar on Planet Hy Man, let alone an Asda. What we have is dried soya, which hits the taste buds like vinegar but apparently is very good for lubricating things. And the market, which looks like a car boot sale compared to Asda. It sells everything needed to live on Planet Hy Man, apart from, well . . . self-respect, a man, and a job.

As for drivers, the leaders got rid of them years ago; we have computer-driven limos for the rich, mopeds which take the legs of a wrestler to pedal-start for the workers, and for the poor, walking.

Watching manually driven cars while under the influence was the height of hilarity for Mex, until an elderly woman sauntered up to the pedestrian crossing and waited. Mex's laughter stopped as she watched the elderly woman wave regally to the drivers.

She mumbled something about leaders and respect. "Should I salute?" she said.

"No, but shutting up might help," said Bunnie.

Christmas Day for Mex was a blur . . .

The rest of us spent Christmas Day tucking into a turkey that had taken days to stuff while watching *The Two Ronnie's*, the Queen's Speech, and Tesco ads. Mex, still unclear of the difference between fudge, toffee, and tablet (she'd worked out what chocolate was), continued to test until the recycle bin was overflowing with empty packets.

Mex was so high she thought the ads were comedies, *The Two Ronnie's* was the news, and the Queen's Speech was messages from above and beyond. She claimed that the Queen and the pedestrian-crossing old woman were not only incognito but "standing on ceremony," which has a whole different meaning on Planet Hy Man.

Mex was, to quote Bunnie, "paranoid."

"They're just elderly," said Bunnie, removing all traces of fudge and the like from the table. "Nothing to fear, dear."

"Fear? Those old dears are the enemy where I come from," said Mex, snatching a fudge from Bunnie.

Mex ripped open the last of the fudge just as the cat, still waiting for its turkey, had enough of sniffing and made a lunge for the table, knocking the Christmas tree into the pyramid of recyclables.

Bunnie, a YouTube fan, shouted at Woody to film.

Woody fumbled for his phone.

While Mex jumped into action, grabbed Bunnie's camera, and, with a "this will confuse the leader," began to film, trailing the cat up the tree, accompanied by the occasional selfie.

The next day, shaking with withdrawals, Mex saw her debut film.

She looked like a maniac.

After her third black coffee, she closed the laptop with disgust, vowing to lay off toffee and fudge—in fact, all sugar—for ninety days. Apparently, it takes that long to break a habit.

None of us saw Bunnie take the laptop away, although I do remember her mumbling something about blackmail; then again, she had been on the whisky.

January 2019—A Trifle Sweet

Woody calls women complicated, but they're not as complicated as Mex's scaling-a-giant-fiber-optic-Christmas-tree-behind-a-cat video.

Bunnie didn't call it complicated, she called it a pile of cat litter. And after Woody explained to me what cat litter was, I tended to agree with her.

Mex had no idea that we had all watched her video. She'd been too busy trying not to think about sugar, dreaming the dreams of an addict. While she'd sweated and shook with only Bunnie's turkey sandwiches to keep her going, we watched her video and Bunnie talked of YouTube.

The festive season is open house season for Bunnie, who claims Hogmanay (New Year) is owned by the Scots.

"A time of seeing out the old and bringing in the new," she said.

"With food, booze, and not only friends who don't stand on ceremony but friends who do."

A ploy, if you ask me, to get rid of the remains of the Christmas turkey, which had made its way into every dish imaginable except perhaps for the trifle.

Turkey is not all it's cracked up to be. In fact, it reminds me of the sort of whiffy soya I often found in Mex's fridge after a week away at rebooting camp.

"Home-cooked food is the key," Bunnie said, rolling handfuls of minced turkey into balls.

Mex was not convinced.

We come from a vegan planet; no one had ever seen a lump of gristle, let alone a pot boiling up a bone. "Stockpots and the like" were "a stock cube too far" for a sober and sugar-free Mex, and she was on the verge of throwing up, until the doorbell rang.

"Get that," Bunnie said to Mex, "and wipe your mouth."

Mex staggered to the door and welcomed, as ordered by Bunnie, the first of the Hogmanay guests.

The elderly man took one look at Mex's flustered face and recognised her from YouTube.

Apparently, videos of cats and Christmas trees are a "hoot" on YouTube. Bunnie had edited and added music and subtitles to Mex's complicated video, turning it into something simple and funny.

"You're the old dear climbing the fiber-optic," laughed another guest with an "excellent."

Mex, with a confused look, offered her a turkey ball, then marched back to the kitchen.

Peering through the steam, she shouted: "What's a fiber-optic?"

Bunnie, pouring herself an extra-large gin, looked up. "Fibroids, hon, the bane of a woman's life—my mother, God rest her soul, could hardly walk because of them."

She sipped.

"No, sorry, that's hemorrhoids. Fibroids are more . . . how do you say . . . *delicate*."

"I see. So climbing them? This is possible?"

Bunnie choked on her gin. "Hardly."

Woody, whose sense of hearing is on par with a sheepdog, stopped mid soup stirring.

"I think she means fiber-optic," he said. "Christmas trees, like what you put on YouTube—Mex's video."

For a moment, Mex stood poised, but the trifle, piled high with whipped cream, almost made her lose her resolve. I could see her finger twitching.

She turned to Bunnie.

"My cat video—you said you'd destroy it, that the world was not ready."

"Destroy? I don't think I said *that*, dear," said Bunnie with a sheepish look.

Mex eyed the trifle and then looked at Bunnie.

"But you're my mentor. You're not supposed to lie, let alone make me look like a fool."

"Honey, you don't need me to make you look like a fool. Besides, I never said anything about mentoring."

"But you've been teaching me things," said Mex.

"Hardly mentoring, more palling about-like."

I could see beads of sweat form at Mex's brow. For the first time in her life, Mex looked like she felt something other than irritation.

I wondered if she would break, crack under the strain of constantly misunderstanding. I watched her hand move closer toward the trifle.

She had watched Bunnie make the custard, even licked the spoon . . .

"Step away from the trifle, ma'am," I said, "custard is not the answer."

Mex caught my eye. She had that look she got when going in for the kill, starting a new mission. She picked up the trifle and took it into the living room—a room now groaning with elderly neighbors talking of the good old days when TV was turned on with a knob and remote controls were things for landing spaceships on the moon.

I could see Mex regain her composure, pull herself together as she plonked the trifle on the table.

"Spaceships on moons," she said, "how very Star Trek."

A splodge of sugary cream dribbled onto the table. Mex, without thinking, lifted it with her finger.

"Stop," I shouted as Woody made a dive for Mex's finger, missing her completely thanks to the cat.

Mex, forefinger poised as cream oozed down the side, said nothing.

"The best thing to do with that," said an elderly gent, "is to lick it. There is nothing a good lick can't fix."

A few of the others chuckled. Mex, however, remained silent; she was at the crossroads of addiction.

"To lick or not to lick," she said, then thrust her hand at the cat and looked at me.

"Once videoed, twice shy," she said.

Confusing pretty much all of the elderly.

THE LADY IN THE BOX

Not all boxes are meant to be opened.

We were sitting in a restaurant in Edinburgh, working our way through a selection of curries as hot as Bunnie's temper, when Woody suggested we carry on to the Edinburgh Festival. My stomach was on fire. I was burning up, sweating, which is not something a robot should do often.

"What is this stuff?" I said.

"It's an Indian," said the blonde at the next table—like that explained everything.

Normally I'd have been enjoying the background music, but I was feeling all tight and crunchy, like one of those packets of crisps. What I needed was a long, lean stretch followed by a position of great twisting that would help my digestion.

Then I heard of the Lady in the Box.

Apparently, there was a lady who could squash herself into a box, and I was curious. I am an Android of great flexibility, a yoga expert, and if a woman can squeeze herself into a box, I want to know about it.

"We've just seen a contortionist," said the blonde at the next table.

"Cartoonist?" said Mex.

"No, contortionist—street performer," said the blonde. "She folds herself up into a square box."

"Whatever for?" muttered Mex.

"And she can twist," said her partner, "into knots that would turn a seaman's hair."

He produced a video that stopped the restaurant and almost put Mex off her jalfrezi.

"All you could see in the end," sniffed the blonde, "was her leotard."

I had to go; I couldn't stand another minute. I wanted to leave, get out into the cool air to trot away my stomach gas and meet this so-called Lady in the Box.

As the blonde gave her partner what for about the seaman comment and Woody explained to Mex the difference between *seamen* and *semen*, I took my chance. I headed for the back door as the waiter appeared, attempting to shut them all up with free mints.

As I entered the festival, I could hear the roar of applause, the drilling of machines mixed with music.

The street was chock-a-block with people, cars, buses, and people speaking languages and accents I had never heard.

I was buzzing off my Teflon tits.

The only music played on Planet Hy Man is the sort of elevator music that puts everyone into a coma, and the only cars we see are driverless limos.

I gazed up at the castle; a piper blasted into the street.

"Am I near the Royal Mile?" I shouted.

"Just around the corner," said the teenager, "you're almost there."

I continued past a magician with a dog, skidded on a leaflet, righted myself on a drunk, ignored the insult, and continued.

It was slow work pushing through the crowds, but I finally made my way onto Mount Pleasant. I passed a seedy-looking man with dreadlocks yelling into the crowd.

"You ain't seen nothing like this, me hearties," he yelled and pulled a bunch of flowers from his pants.

"Jesus!" muttered someone.

I walked on: past two men playing drums, past a dark man in a duffel coat sniffing into a bottle in a bag.

"Pound for coffee?" he said.

I gestured to my empty pockets, then, reading the brown man's upright-middle-finger gesture, quickly moved on.

The street was lined with performers competing for the attention of the crowd; it was hard to keep moving. I ended up sandwiched between a young girl lamenting about men in general and an elderly woman moaning about her bunions, right in front of a man wriggling about in a locked straitjacket.

"Let me tell you a story," grunted the performer, "of Alcatraz and my escape."

The crowd muttered and jolted forward. I was about to move on when I heard a loud rumble. I turned to see a large, hairy, masked juggler posing with a chainsaw.

The sound drowned out everything.

"Alcatraz the inescapable," shouted the escapologist.

The juggler tossed the chainsaw into the air. The crowd gasped as he caught the saw with his thick muscular arms.

The escapologist, watching his audience dwindle, nodded to his sidekick, who wheeled out a unicycle . . .

"Alcatraz, oh Alcatraz, the place where no bird sings."

The crowd was silent as he leveraged himself onto the unicycle, his arms still twisted in the straitjacket. He was a whisper of a man with a thin ponytail and birdlike features, which at the moment were pinched with discomfort as he balanced on the unicycle.

The older woman cheered, bunions (I assume) forgotten.

"This is way better than the Lady in the Box," she said. "I mean how long can you stare at a box?"

"Is she still there?" I said.

"Oh yes, she's still there, with a sidekick for comedy."

"Comedy in a box?" said someone from behind. "Hardly call it that."

I marched up the steep hill of Cockburn Street, past more food shops and the smell of waffles, chocolate, and chips.

"You see the lady? The one in the box?"

"Aye, something else."

"Where?"

The young man whistled through his teeth. "Just keep going. Ignore the comedian, he's as funny as herpes."

The street was lined with tables and chairs, people sitting and talking, artists drawing or manipulating balloons into weird shapes.

I pushed through the crowd, skidded to a stop, and stared at the Perspex box. Her limbs folded about her body—all I could see was her leotard.

"Come see the impossible," shouted the comedian, "a woman who can tie herself into knots any seaman would be proud of."

Nobody laughed, that is, until I caught the comedian's eye.

Full of curry, desperate for a twist and fold to sort my rumbling tum, I shouted, "Bring me a smaller box and I'll show you a few knots a seaman has never *heard* of!"

The box shuddered as her bright pink legs moved; then a hand appeared, followed by a shoulder and pink hair . . .

Like a cat in a shoebox, the Lady in the Box peeked out.

"Seaman?" she said. "Did someone say seaman?"

"He did," the comedian said, pointing to me.

"He did," I said, pointing to the comedian.

She looked from me to the comedian. "What have seamen to do with my box?"

"It's all about the knots," muttered the comedian with an uncomfortable shuffle.

"It was but a mere joke," I added.

The Lady in the Box, who went by the name of Matilda, eased herself out and sat on the edge. Once unfolded, she looked a lot older, more a gran's vintage than a granddaughter's.

The crowd looked disappointed. Her stick-thin body, when squashed into the box, had men gaping and drooling. Now, unfolded in a wrinkled bodysuit (not the best Lycra I had seen), the Lady in the Box seemed frail rather than elusive.

She eyed me and, with a small cough, demanded to know where my "spot" was.

"Spot?"

"Yes." She gestured to my golden suit. "I mean what are you? One of those boring statues, standing like you have no feet? Hardly talent. I mean you try squeezing yourself into that box five times a day with last night's vindaloo making itself known."

"Vindaloo?" muttered a voice from the crowd.

"You eat vindaloo before squeezing?" muttered another voice.

"Jesus," chuckled the comedian. "Glad I'm standing upwind."

"Well, it's that or dhal, beggars can't be choosers," snapped Matilda, now completely out of the box. "What do you expect when you get free accommodation above an Indian? Fine dining? Cordon bleu chicken?"

"Thought you were a vegetarian," said the comedian.

"I am when I can afford it," she huffed. Matilda glared at her audience. "People don't throw money like they used to."

A few men shuffled.

"It's not easy making a living when you're competing with"—Matilda eyed me—"statues and fire-eaters."

"You stay above an Indian?" said a man coming forth with a few coins.

"What did you expect, the Hilton?" she said with a thank-you nod.

A few more coins appeared.

"I keep the toilets clean, serve a few poppadums, and I get a free room and all the mistaken orders you can shake a stick at."

"You serve in a restaurant," said an elderly woman, "at your age? You poor thing." She nudged her husband, who, with a grunt, slid a note under a pile of brown change.

"And whoever threw these two p's in should be ashamed of themselves," she snapped.

"It was me," said a tiny boy.

The crowd was silent. In the distance, we could hear the hissing of fire-eating followed by the roar of applause.

A young man appeared, placed a fiver on the coat, and retrieved a couple of coins, muttering about the parking meter. His partner nudged him.

"Ken, must you?"

"What?"

"She's eating the wrong orders."

"Wrong orders my arse," he sniffed.

"Last night I was forced to eat burnt chapattis," said Matilda, now poised on the edge of her box.

"And what's that to do with me?" said Ken. He turned to his partner. "She bounced into the box, wasn't even there a minute, and bounced back out again. Hardly a show. She's lucky she got a pound, if you ask me."

The Lady in the Box sniffed. "Well, I could bounce back in if you like, or perhaps you'd like to do a little bouncing"—she glared—"for your parking meter."

The comedian looked at me.

I looked at him.

He gestured to the box.

"Permit me, ma'am; I believe two for the price of one may boost your sales and avail you of some vegetarian cuisine of the non-spicy variety."

She, with a knock-yourself-out gesture, stood back.

I handed my gloves to the old lady and my shoes to the comedian (ignoring his face-pulling), tossed my jacket at Ken, and stepped into the box.

With great ease, I began the process of folding.

The crowd hushed apart from Ken, who, with reverent folding of my coat, shouted, "Come on, my son."

Matilda's foot inched in and we, without a grunt, shuffled as her butt ended up near my cheek.

The crowd oohed and aahed as coins landed with a thump on her jacket.

I eased myself into a banana around the other body position, my head squished into a corner.

"Now pose," she whispered into the small of my back.

I peered out of my corner and smiled, face flattened by the Perspex, giving a squashed thumbs-up.

The crowd began to cheer, clap, shout, "More!"

Then I heard another whisper . . .

"It was all rubbish about the vindaloo," she said. "I stay at my granddaughter's. We take it in turns—it's a family business."

"Business?" I muttered, smile fixed.

"Don't even like curries," she said. "I'm more a Chinese woman."

THE POLISHING OF A KNOB

A knob by any other name still requires a hand to work it.

"February is a month never spoken about on Planet Hy Man," I said to Bunnie.

Bunnie, a master of multitasking, was spring cleaning *and* listening, while Mex was sitting on the couch, feet up, trying to get to grips with the *Radio Times*.

Bunnie muttered a "hmmm."

"We used to celebrate it when men were more than footmen and enjoyed festivals, dressing up, and coming home to a woman pleased to see them," I said. "Back in the days when automation was on the cusp of existence."

"March, on the other hand, is a month of cleaning," muttered Mex.

"And what the hell is a footman?" said Bunnie, working up a shine on the TV screen.

"March," I continued, "is a month of celebration for us on Planet Hy Man. It is the anniversary of the first egg fertilization and the beginning of the end for men and their stupid festivals."

"It's celebrated by wearing giant Petri dishes on one's head," muttered Mex, turning the magazine upside down. The *TV Guide* really threw her.

Bunnie stopped. "What?"

"And for those who can't afford a Petri dish, anything that looks like a large Petri dish," I said.

"Aye right," muttered Bunnie, returning to her polishing.

"A month where women are 'tickled pink' and spring into action at the drop of a hat," I said.

"Or pertinent dish, if you want to get technical," said Mex with a flick of a page.

"You're taking the piss," said Bunnie.

"The first day of March is spent filling one's Petri dish with freebies. The markets are free, and the lower-level Building of Opulence is open to all."

"Women go crazy," muttered Mex.

"I find that hard to believe," said Bunnie.

"And create such a mess that it takes the rest of the month to clean up," I said.

"March is a month hated by the cleaning team," muttered Mex, rotating the magazine with a confused look.

Bunnie stopped in her tracks. "Wait a minute—you have a building called Opulence?"

"Well, yes," I said.

"Why would you call a building Opulence?" said Bunnie.

"Figure of speech, ma'am."

"It's more a statement," said Mex, tossing the magazine aside with disinterest.

"Of what?"

"Well, opulence—it's not available for everyone, I guess," said Mex.

Bunnie admired her polished TV. "Yes, we all know that," she said, flicking imaginary dust from the top. "But what is opulence in your world?"

"How would I know?" muttered Mex.

Bunnie looked at her.

"Anything that is in the building of opulence, ma'am," I said.

"And what is that?" said Bunnie.

"I don't know," sighed Mex. "I have only been to the room with a view for orders. I am not a Voted In. I am only allowed up the back entrance."

Bunnie moved on to polishing the door. Surveying the finger marks, she let Izzie in.

"I have spent the last month trying to understand a world where men are footmen, whatever that is."

"Men who stand to attention, ma'am, and retrieve things, sort of like a . . . retriever," I muttered.

Bunnie eyed me with the sort of look she called cryptic. "Really?"

Izzie barked and jumped up on Mex's lap, his favourite place.

Mex cooed. "We don't have dogs on Planet Hy Man, ma'am," she said.

"That explains a lot, except . . ." Bunnie eyed Mex, who was talking gibberish to Izzie.

"You're the great man spy who rid Planet Hy Man of all men," said Bunnie, "kicked them out."

"More kicked to the gym, ma'am," I said.

"You made it all possible though," Bunnie said to Mex.

"Well, yes," said Mex.

"Why the back entrance then?" said Bunnie.

"The Voted In are easily impressed," I said to Bunnie. "Their idea of opulence is anything others can't afford."

"And?" said Bunnie.

"And Mex and the like choose what to make unaffordable," I said. "It keeps them happy, malleable."

"Who's a cute boy?" Mex cooed at Izzie.

"Insightful," muttered Bunnie.

"Turns out it doesn't matter if it's males or females who rule. They are all the same in the end," I said.

"I see," tutted Bunnie.

"Manipulatable," muttered Mex.

"What some would call a knob," said Bunnie, now polishing one.

Mex and I, confused, looked at each other until Bunnie gave a way-too-in-depth description of the true meaning of a knob, where, as she put it, polishing was negotiable.

"So, *the polishing of a knob*," I said, "is a term best kept in the same sentence as a duster."

"Or Mr. Clean." She chuckled.

"On our planet," muttered Mex, "polishing is strictly for the robots."

THE FOOT RUB

The rubbing of a foot can lead to many things.

DBO was sitting in the shed having her "feet sorted" by a footman young enough to sit in a squatting fashion without hurting his bunions. She was twenty-three with no idea about sex, one-night stands, or massages, and as the footman rubbed her feet, she looked on with confusion.

She had been told by many that touching was barbaric . . .

Her feet had never been discussed, touched, or even looked at before, and here she was having them caressed, washed, and talked about by a footman with paper-thin skin, loose folds about his neck, and hands as soft as tofu butter . . .

"Tough spot, ma'am."

"Could do with a little moisture."

"A better-fitting shoe wouldn't go astray."

The footman, it seemed, had a lot to say about feet.

DBO smiled as he got stuck into her heel. "Bit more," she finally muttered.

"Ma'am, we have another twenty minutes left; do you *really* want me to remain in one spot?"

"Twenty minutes? I don't understand."

"Time limit," he muttered. "There is only so much pleasure a woman can take . . ."

She wondered, "Do you do ankles?"

"Ankles are permitted, as are calves and knees, especially the back of them."

"Oh?"

No one had told her about the back of things . . . then she wondered what else she had not been told about.

"Yes, ma'am, there is the back of things and the front," the footman muttered under his limp mustache. "We see them all but are not permitted to comment."

When the footman first entered the shed, DBO's nerves hit a new height and she wondered if her goose, albeit tofu, was cooked. The only time a footman walked anywhere near the shed was to spy.

DBO had been hiding under the stairs at the time, contemplating her next course of action, when she heard a muffled scuffle. She spied the footman clumsily squeezing through the vent, knocking the roto clipboard off its peg. She watched as he squeezed himself in, pulled himself up.

She had no idea what to say, as she had never been alone with a footman before, but she knew she had to do something. He was heading for her hiding place.

She coughed.

He started.

"Foot rub, ma'am," he said.

She was totally thrown. "Rub? What is that?"

"What's good for the goose is good for the gander," he muttered with no reference to tofu. Then, before she had a chance to ask what a gander had to do with things, he laid her leg onto his knee, slipped off her shoe, and pulled out a tube of lubricant.

The scent of hemp mingled with the smell of damp knocked her off guard.

She looked at the top of the footman's bald head as lubricant squelched through her toes. Feet had never been discussed in the past; no one ever mentions the joy of a foot rub. The only thing she knew about foot massage was her granny-spa foot bath which bubbled over the sides, making a mess, and a scraper which, once engaged, caused so much pain that DBO never mentioned calluses again, even in jest.

The footman moved to the other foot and began with her big toe. He twirled it around and then ran his fingers along the joint. His hands were warm and oily; she sighed.

"Why have we never heard of this?" she said.

"Those higher up," said the footman, working his way along her arch.

"What?"

"The Voted In, they banned it—for all except for themselves. Apparently, sitting about a big table is hard on one's feet."

DBO detected a smirk. *Was that a hint of sarcasm?*

She sighed. He'd found that spot again . . . releasing feelings she had no idea she had.

Focus . . . focus . . . remember, there are spies everywhere.

"This Legless," she finally said. "Have you heard of him?"

"Everyone has heard of him."

"Did you meet him?"

"I rowed a stationary beside him; never seen anyone pedal like him. That man was a genius—with so little work, he achieved so much. Apparently it was all in the push."

"Ooh, rub that a little bit harder . . . go on."

"All us men took riding a stationary for granted back then. It seemed easy, just a matter of pedaling, but somehow Legless took it to a new level; according to him, it was the quality of the push that mattered."

DBO knew nothing about stationaries except that they were old-fashioned energy providers modelled on the outdated bike, which, thanks to the lack of dirt track upkeep, were as useful as a shed without a door.

She, like all shed workers, had a moped, which was also as useless as the doorless shed. Starting it took pedaling on a grand scale, and getting it to stop required jumping off. In fact, her moped hadn't been used since she'd jumped off it in front of the shed and it had continued, knocking through the front door, smashing the only window the shed had, and disrupting the so-called "beverage corner."

It had taken her all day to sort that mess out.

"Pushing," said the footman, "is beyond the realm of language and is not as easy as it looks."

"I have been told that; all men say that."

"And when was the last time you rode a stationary?" said the footman.

"I drive a moped," she said. "Ever tried one of those?"

"No, ma'am; they are too mechanical for the likes of us men, requiring multitasking, a talent we are apparently not qualified for . . . although I have heard starting one is a nightmare."

She wondered if he was taking the proverbial. "You sure you're not a robot?"

"Why, ma'am?"

"You talk like one." She was about to say more when she noted something in his pocket. She looked closer. *What is that?*

Words from DBO's gran flashed back to her: "Real footmen are silent—beware of those that speak . . ."

DBO stared at the footman. "What is that in your pocket?"

He sat back from her foot, pulling a lace hanky from his pocket; a note fluttered out.

DBO picked it up. She read it, then looked at the footman. "I thought Legless was dead."

"That's what they all say," he said.

DBO looked at him.

"Those higher up," he said, "which is pretty much everyone, in your case."

DBO slipped her shoes on. "It says here that he is not only alive and kicking but has a plan?"

"That is the gist of it, ma'am."

She stood up; her toes slid down to the front. She pulled an "ouch" face.

"Did warn ma'am about the quality of one's shoe," said the footman.

"Quality of my shoe? I work in a shed on pay so low it doesn't exist. I can't afford shampoo, let alone shoes; I had to wait about the recycle bins to get these."

The footman looked at her with an *I find that hard to believe* look and sniffed. "Best to wait for the lubricant to be absorbed." He looked at her. "There is time."

"Time?" said DBO. "I have no time; the planet is relying on me to save things."

"Yes, but without your moped, how can you get home, let alone save things?"

"You're too smart for your own good," she snapped. "You think you can bamboozle me with your fancy oils and talk of time."

"Ma'am, the last thing on my mind is bamboozlement. Besides, Legless hasn't finished sorting your moped yet. You are, after all, part of his plan."

This is a work of fiction. Similarities to real people, places, or events are entirely coincidental.

A Dress For a Queen and Other Stories

First edition May 09, 2020.
Copyright © 2020 Kerrie Noor.
Written by Kerrie Noor.

❀ Created with Vellum

ABOUT THE AUTHOR

Back in the days before TV had remote controls and Scotland was known for the Bay City Rollers, Kerrie left Australia on a working holiday and fell in love with many things Scottish, including a man and Panto.

After years of performing, Kerrie decided to write some of her experiences down in a series of short stories and plans to write more; along with her Belly Dancing and Beyond series and soon to be published comic sci-fi series.

If you would like to find out more, please feel free to visit-
http://kerrienoor.com
https://www.bookbub.com/authors/kerrie-noor
Cheers and Regards
Kerrie Noor